Felicia slowly opened her eyes to find Griffin staring at her, specifically her mouth.

"Sorry. I've got a thing for good food," she explained as she took another bite.

"I think I have a thing for watching you enjoy it." His voice had taken on a husky tone.

Their eyes collided. Griffin put down his fork, pushed back his chair and stood. Felicia's gaze followed his every movement. He came to stand next to her. "Put your fork down," he ordered. Felicia complied, trembling slightly with anticipation.

Griffin pulled back her chair, took Felicia's hand and drew her in his arms. The sudden movement made her grip his broad shoulders as she raised her head slightly to maintain eye contact.

"You are simply breathtaking, and I can't wait a second longer to do this."

Griffin leaned forward slowly, keeping his eyes on Felicia's as he ran his tongue across her lips before capturing them in a passionate kiss.

The kiss whipped Felicia's body into a raging, out-of-control inferno, an overwhelmingly unique experience for her.

Dear Reader,

I can hardly believe we've come to the end of this exciting voyage. When I started The Blake Sisters series, I wanted to introduce the world to three dynamic women. I'm so very pleased that the first two sisters have been so well received. You've seen glimpses of the third sister, and now it's time to bring you her full story.

In *Tempting the Heiress*, old medical-school friends Felicia and Griffin struggle to determine the best way to raise the child that has suddenly been placed in their care, all while fighting their long-buried desire for each other. Watching these friends struggle to become parents and lovers is exhilarating.

I love interacting with readers, so please let me know how you enjoyed Felicia and Griffin's story. You can contact me on Facebook or Twitter. I hope to bring you more exciting and very sexy stories in the near future.

Until then,

Martha

TEMPTING *the* HEIRESS

MARTHA KENNERSON

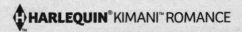
HARLEQUIN® KIMANI™ ROMANCE

Recycling programs
for this product may
not exist in your area.

ISBN-13: 978-0-373-86468-3

Tempting the Heiress

Copyright © 2016 by Martha Kennerson

For questions and comments about the quality of this book please contact us
at CustomerService@Harlequin.com.

Printed in U.S.A.

Martha Kennerson's love of reading and writing is a significant part of who she is, and she uses both to create the kinds of stories that touch your heart. Martha lives with her family in League City, Texas, and believes her current blessings are only matched by the struggle it took to achieve such happiness. To find out more about Martha and her journey, check out her website at marthakennerson.com.

Books by Martha Kennerson

Harlequin Kimani Romance

Protecting the Heiress
Seducing the Heiress
Tempting the Heiress

Visit the Author Profile page at Harlequin.com for more titles.

This book is dedicated to all the readers
who have traveled this journey with me and love
the Blake sisters as much as I do. You're all amazing,
and I really appreciate your unyielding support.

Acknowledgments

I'd like to thank my husband for
his willingness to share me with so many crazy characters.
Love you, honey.

Chapter 1

After a long day of traveling, an exhausted Dr. Felicia Blake, wearing blue jeans and a white T-shirt, her long, curly hair up in a messy bun, made her way through the busy Hartsfield–Jackson Atlanta International Airport. As the third-born of the beautiful, highly accomplished Blake triplets and heir to her family's billion-dollar international security firm, Felicia was one of the brilliant physicians working for the CIA as a medical research scientist specializing in biochemistry.

Felicia often found herself traveling the world, chasing down many different types of deadly diseases to learn their origin. While Felicia loved the time she spent working in South Korea, she was happy to be back in the United States.

Felicia had just cleared customs and was waiting to collect her bag when she overheard two young women talking. The taller of the two said, "Girl, I'm telling you he's got to be."

"How do you know he's a celebrity?" her friend replied, giving her the side-eye.

"Celebrities love coming to the ATL," she said, snapping her fingers twice in the air. "Look at the way he's dressed. Anyway, he's *too* fine not to be famous."

Both women laughed.

Felicia's natural curiosity got the best of the good doctor. She raised her head and scanned the area where the two women were staring. Felicia's eyes collided with a uniquely stunning but very familiar set of gray eyes. "Griffin," she murmured. Felicia stood staring at the only man that had ever touched her heart but never knew it. He'd challenged Felicia to go beyond her own perceived limits, while making the shy young woman feel safe enough to open up and let others get to know her. Griffin had taught Felicia how to manage different types of relationships, and that growth had helped her become a better doctor. Felicia hadn't realized just how much she'd missed their friendship until now. Felicia's mind flashed back to the first moment they'd met...

Thinking she was running late to her first medical school lecture, Felicia ran down the hall and into the room only to find the most handsome, bronze-skinned man she'd ever seen. He was sitting in the front row, slouched in a theater-style chair, long legs stretched out before him, his eyes closed. His finely trimmed beard, short hair and perfect physique reminded her of someone that belonged in the pages of *GQ* magazine instead of a classroom for those who aspired to become doctors.

"Excuse me, I don't mean to disturb you, but is this Dr. Jacobson's microbiology class?"

"Yes," he responded without moving or opening his eyes.

"Then where is everyone?" Felicia asked, scanning the empty room, wondering if she'd missed something.

The gorgeous man sighed deeply, tilted his head toward her and slowly opened his eyes. Felicia offered what she hoped was a friendly smile.

The man sat up slowly as his gaze roamed her body while still not bothering to answer the question.

"This is Dr. Jacobson's Tuesday microbiology class, right?" Felicia asked again, checking the schedule she held. His open stare caused her to look down at her outfit to ensure she hadn't worn the wrong color scrubs or wonder if her messy, high ponytail might have been too much so.

He nodded and Felicia shifted her weight from one leg to the other and bit her bottom lip, a habit she was trying to break. "The class got pushed back by forty-five minutes. Didn't you get the text?"

Felicia rummaged in her backpack, came up empty, shook her head. "I left my phone in my room."

"I'm Griffin Kaile, by the way," he said, standing and walking slowly toward her. "Third year."

Felicia's breath caught and her heart skipped several beats with each step he took. "I—I'm…I'm Felicia Blake, first year," she replied, offering her hand and staring up into a beautiful set of gray eyes. "Pleased to meet you."

"Trust me, the pleasure is all mine," he said, holding her gaze as he took her hand and gave it a small shake.

The moment he touched her, a charge went through Felicia's body unlike anything she'd ever felt before…

The women's laughter brought Felicia back to the present, where she stood and stared at the gorgeous figure from her past. A dazzlingly handsome blend of his African-American and Chinese-American heritages, he was the only man who would have been capable of making Felicia reconsider where she would be starting her career after medical school.

Dr. Griffin Kaile Jr., a tall, athletically built, outstandingly gifted cardiovascular surgeon and sole heir to his family's billion-dollar multimedia conglomerates, stood with his arms folded across his chest in front of the baggage carousel, wearing a black suit that was cut perfectly for his frame, when his cell phone rang. He reached into his jacket pocket, retrieved the phone and read the screen.

"Kaile," Griffin answered.

"Kaile, it's Mel. You back in town?"

"Just. What's up?" Griffin asked.

"You headed home?" Mel inquired.

"After I stop by the hospital."

"Cool, I just have a few test results I need you to take a look at," Mel said.

"Anything urgent?" Griffin asked.

"Really? Don't you trust that your brilliant physician's assistant would hit you up if there were something critical for you to handle?"

"Of course I do. Otherwise you wouldn't be my brilliant physician's assistant," Griffin replied, his tone flat.

No matter how necessary it may have been or how talented his team members were, Griffin struggled with delegating anything he believed was ultimately his responsibility. As an only child, Griffin had never mastered the art of sharing.

"How did it go? Did you get to meet with everyone?" Mel's voice escalated slightly.

"Yes, and they all seem extremely capable," Griffin confirmed.

"Capable? Those are some of the best fellows in the country and they're all chomping at the bit to come work for you, and you call them capable," he said, laughing. "Have you decided which two you're going to pick?"

"Not yet. I'll decide by the end of the week. See you in a while."

Griffin was putting away his phone when he felt a pair of eyes on him. The child of successful public figures who were also media moguls, he was used to often-unwanted attention; only this time something felt different. Griffin's eyes snapped up and lased in on his target. His heart raced as his eyes were held captive by the most beautiful woman he'd ever seen. "Can't be," Griffin whispered to himself.

Griffin stood staring at the only woman he'd ever really wanted but could never have. The woman he often thought about—still fantasized about…and compared others to—was standing mere feet away. As if he'd been polarized by a magnet, Griffin felt himself being drawn forward. She was a physically fit, olive-skinned beauty with high cheekbones, luxuriously long jet-black hair and a heart-shaped face bestowed on her by her parents—an Italian mother and African-American and Hispanic father.

"Felicia… Felicia Blake," she heard a baritone voice call, her heart skipping several beats. Felicia bit her bottom lip and nodded slowly. Still not sure she wasn't imagining that her long-lost love was coming toward her, Felicia looked to the two women standing next to her for confirmation. Their wide and flirtatious smiles were all the affirmation she needed.

First, Felicia was summoned to Atlanta to receive some mysterious bequest from her late best friend from medical school, and now she came face-to-face with her favorite lab partner and secret crush.

"Dr. Griffin Kaile," Felicia said, pulling herself together. "It's been a while… Six years."

"Yes, it has, and you haven't changed a bit. You look amazing," he said, smiling.

Felicia looked down at her outfit and frowned. "Not really, but thanks. You look…professional."

Griffin smirked. "Thanks."

Professional. Really, Felicia? "How have you been?" she asked, breaking eye contact when she spied the gift from her sisters—red Valextra Avietta luggage—making its way down the carousel's runway. Felicia reached for the large wheeled trolley.

"I got it," Griffin said, placing his hand over hers.

Griffin's touch sent a charge through her body that she'd only felt one other time before, delivered by the same man. Felicia quickly pulled her hand from his and took a step back. "I'm doing well." Griffin picked up the large bag and placed it next to Felicia before reaching for his own leather suitcase.

"What a gentleman," Felicia heard the two women say.

"Thanks," Felicia said, smiling up at Griffin.

"Last I heard, you were working somewhere overseas," Griffin said.

Felicia nodded. "I've spent the last year working in Asia."

"Wow, I bet that was an adventure. Are you in town long? We should get together…catch up," Griffin suggested, the corners of his mouth rising slowly.

"I…I'd really like that, but I'm only in town for the day. Unexpected and urgent business I have to tend to."

"I can't convince you to extend your trip?" Griffin asked, offering her a wide smile.

"You can convince me of anything," the shorter of the two women offered, not bothering to hide her eavesdropping.

Felicia smirked at the unsolicited commentary. "I wish I could, but my family is sending the plane for me right after my meeting. If I'm not on it, there will be hell to pay. I haven't seen them in a while."

"I understand. Do you have a card?" Griffin asked, reaching into his pocket and pulling out one of his own. "Here is mine. It has my home number on it, too."

"Sorry, I haven't had much use for cards in the last year," she said, accepting his.

"Well—"

"Excuse me, sir," a tall man dressed in hospital scrubs interrupted. "The car is here."

"Thanks, Doug. I'll be right there," Griffin replied before turning his attention back to Felicia. "When you get settled, give me a call. I'd really like to hear what you've been up to," he reiterated.

"Sure."

"It really was great seeing you again." Griffin smiled, picked up his bag and headed toward the exit.

"'Sure'? Could you be a bigger geek?" Felicia chastised herself.

"Nope," the two women said, laughing as they left with their bags in hand.

Felicia's shoulders dropped. Even after all these years and her many accomplishments, Griffin could still turn Felicia's brain to mush and make her weak in the knees. Griffin was one of the few people Felicia had been closest to during her tenure at medical school. While Felicia had been the youngest in their group of friends, a twenty-year-old first-year student, he'd never treated her as though she was lesser in any way, and she would always be grateful for that.

Running into Griffin today of all days was such a real, serendipitous moment that Felicia couldn't help but wonder if it might mean something. She extended the handle on her travel trolley and made her way toward the exit. Felicia spotted a driver holding a sign with her name on it. "Excuse me, I'm Dr. Felicia Blake."

The driver removed his hat and offered up a quick nod. "I'm Jeff from Atlanta Limousine Express," he said, introducing himself before reaching for her bag. "Follow me. We're right outside."

Jeff led Felicia through a set of double glass doors and she was immediately hit by the bright sunlight. She reached into her purse and removed another must-have gift from her sisters—a pair of Chanel sunglasses. "Do you know where we're going?" Felicia asked, placing the glasses over her squinted eyes.

"Yes, ma'am. The downtown law offices of McCormick and Associates," he recited.

Felicia stopped at the sight of the large black vehicle. "What in the world…"

"The person requesting the car asked for the Sprinter Limo Coach," he explained.

Felicia's forehead creased. "The what?"

"A limousine-style van. I was told you'd need privacy and room to change." Jeff's eyes scanned her attire.

"Farrah." Felicia looked down at herself again. "I guess I *should* freshen up a bit."

"Yes, ma'am. We'll be there in about thirty minutes," he explained, helping her into the van.

Chapter 2

"Welcome back," Mel greeted, entering the executive doctor's lounge holding an electronic tablet, where he found Griffin standing in the kitchenette, staring down into his coffee cup, obviously lost in his thoughts.

I can't believe she was standing right in front of me and I actually let her get away...again. But it's not like I had much of a choice. Why couldn't she give me one day? She's not married. Maybe she's seeing someone. Get a grip. Why are you tripping over someone you haven't seen in years who's still not interested?

"Hello..." Mel waved his hand in front of Griffin's face.

"What's up?" Griffin frowned at Mel.

"What's up...what's up with you?"

"Nothing. I assume those—" he gestured at the tablet with his coffee cup "—are the charts and test results you want me to review."

"Yes, and please tell me that's not the last cup of English breakfast tea you're having."

Griffin's eyebrows came to attention. "When have you ever seen me drink tea?" Griffin replied, tossing the empty K-cup in the trash. "What happened to the old coffeepot?"

"It's been retired." Mel handed Griffin the tablet and went in search of the tea K-cups.

Griffin accepted the tablet, took his coffee and avoided the leather sofa and chairs in favor of a seat at the conference table, where he started flipping through the charts.

"So…" Mel said, taking a seat across from Griffin at the conference table.

"So…what?" Griffin replied, not bothering to raise his head as he continued to read through the charts.

"Who was the woman at the airport?" he asked before taking a sip of his tea.

Griffin raised his head and frowned. "How did you…? Doug. Damn, gossip sure travels fast around this place."

"Of course. The women at this hospital, and all the surrounding hospitals, for that matter, love chasing after you. They want to know if you're off the market. Hell, the men around here do, too. Maybe if you are, some of these women will give the rest of us a shot," he explained, laughing.

Griffin's phone beeped, indicating he'd received a text. "Man, please. You get just as much attention as I do," he reminded his friend as he checked the incoming message.

"True, but who was she?" Mel pressed.

A wide smile crawled across Griffin's face. "Just an old friend."

"*Just.* By that stupid look on your face, she's not *just* anything."

True. She could have been the one. We were perfect for each other; the best of friends. Becoming lovers was the next natural step. Too bad she couldn't see it.

Griffin sat back in his chair and took a drink of his coffee. He knew his friend and colleague was right; Felicia wasn't just anyone. "She's this brilliant doctor that's—"

"Beautiful, from what I hear."

Griffin nodded slowly. "That she is, but she's so much more." He took another sip of his coffee.

Mel slid his empty cup away from him. "She coming... or going?"

"I thought Doug told you. I saw her collecting her baggage, so she was obviously coming into town."

"That's not what I mean." Mel scratched his head.

"Well, what do you mean?" Griffin asked, turning his attention back to the tablet.

"Is she coming or going from your life?" Mel clarified.

Griffin met his friend's eyes, his face void of expression. "I don't see Mrs. Cartwright's CT scan results here."

Mel smirked. "Okay, I get it. It's none of my business. Her results weren't ready," he said, standing. "I'll go check again."

"That would be great." Once the door closed behind Mel, Griffin stood and stared out the window. He thought again about what Mel had asked and said, "That's a damn good question."

Felicia sat with her legs crossed at her ankles, taking in her surroundings and feeling very grateful that her sister had made arrangements so she could change into her gray pencil skirt and gray-and-white blouse, something much more appropriate for her meeting. The Andy Warhol painting and Persian rugs in the immaculately decorated lobby of the law offices of McCormick and Associates screamed sophisticated wealth.

"Dr. Blake? John McCormick." A sandy-haired man, medium-built, introduced himself, offering his hand. "I hope I haven't kept you waiting long."

"No, not at all, and it's Felicia," she said, accepting his hand.

"All right, Felicia, and I am John. Please come in."

Felicia followed John into his office. The large mahogany desk that was placed in the center of the room sat in front of a large window and was surrounded by wall-to-wall law books, several of which she recognized from Farrah's office. A long leather sofa sat to the right of the desk, a wooden, glass-topped bar by its side. Felicia took a seat in one of the high-backed leather chairs that faced his desk. John took a seat behind his desk and pulled out a thick file folder from his desk drawer.

"Are you sure I can't get you anything to drink? Coffee... water?"

"No, thank you," she replied, tamping down her impatience. "I'd just really like to know what this is all about. I don't understand why Valerie would give me anything, let alone make me the sole beneficiary to her estate." Her brows knit together. "We haven't seen each other in years. Our careers went in different directions, and mine taking me halfway across the world made the Sunday brunch catch-up sessions we talked about having after graduation impossible. I haven't even spoken to her since she and Harry got married."

John's face was tense. "I understand you have questions and I'll do my best to explain as much as I can." John exhaled. "About a year ago, Valerie came to me for help."

Felicia leaned forward in her chair. "What kind of help?" she asked, a tad of curiosity coursing through her. "Sorry, I'll let you finish."

John's mouth twisted up. "She wanted me to redraft her will. Something she'd been planning ever since she'd received that settlement from Harry after their divorce. Well, as part of that process, she told me a rather interesting story."

"Like what?"

"You were aware of her several bouts with ovarian cancer, bouts that she overcame, right?" he asked, his oval-shaped face void of expression.

"Yes, of course."

"And you were part of the group of friends that helped her through her first recovery?"

"That's true," she said.

"I understand you all organized blood drives, donated hair for wigs. and some even participated in a couple more dramatic actions, like the guys making sperm donations."

Felicia offered a small smile as bittersweet memories came to mind. She wondered what the efforts of several of their friends had to do with the present. "We were young medical students…impulsive, I guess. But that was such a long time ago. What does any of that have to do with whatever this is about?"

"Everything, actually. You see, someone's act of kindness was taken advantage of, and I'm here to make things right," he confessed. "As right as I can, anyway."

Felicia's frown deepened. "How so?"

"By making sure my client's wishes are adhered to without anyone getting hurt, especially you."

"Me? What are you talking about?" Felicia said as an uneasy feeling besieged her, much like when she had to deliver bad news to world leaders.

"I'm going to make sure that what Valerie wants you to have remains yours. Her bequest is rightfully yours on every level."

Felicia questioned, "Rightfully mine?"

"I'd better start from the beginning. After the divorce and that large sum of money landed in her account, Valerie was ready to start a new life. She finally had the financial freedom to do it, too."

Felicia offered a knowing nod. "She always wanted that, to have the ability to afford to do and go wherever she wanted."

"Growing up in the foster care system is hard on anyone, but for Valerie it just seems like it was especially rough on her, although she rarely talked about it with me," John said, pushing the folder to the side.

"With me, either. She always said what happened, happened, and it's best to let skeletons stay buried." Felicia felt an overwhelming sense of sorrow for her friend, who'd died two months ago. While that was not unusual, she hated that the cancer Valerie had once beaten had taken her old friend. Felicia sat in silence while John continued.

"In spite of the divorce, Valerie wanted to become a mother. She wanted to have a child to share her new life with," he said with a hint of sadness in his voice. "Her career was going well. She had her health, so she just knew this was the next logical step for herself, even if she had to do it alone."

"She was always fearless like that," Felicia offered.

"Do you remember when Valerie went to that reproductive clinic and had her eggs harvested and stored?"

"It was just before her first chemo and radiation treatments started." Felicia's remorse was mounting. "She wanted to make sure she could have her own children. Valerie spent every dime she'd earned that summer before, as well as the money she'd made from the two jobs she'd held, just to pay for the procedure. She refused any help I offered."

John scratched his head. "Unfortunately, when Valerie went back to the clinic to have her eggs fertilized and implanted, she found out that only four were viable, which meant she only had two shots at having her own child."

"Oh, no, I bet she was devastated. Valerie had been adamant about having a biological child. But transferring two good embryos into her uterus at her age would give a forty to fifty percent chance that at least one embryo would result in a live birth." Felicia released a pained sigh. "She wanted a baby that looked like her, a connection that she herself never had."

"That's putting it mildly. The clinic went through a lot of changes after Dr. Dan Ambrose took over."

"Dan Ambrose?" she asked, swiping at a piece of hair that had fallen into her eyes. "I don't recognize the name, but I've been working out of the country these past couple of years."

"He's a fertility specialist that became the clinic's administrator about four years ago. When Valerie found out she only had a couple of chances at making her dreams come true, she took matters into her own hands to ensure she had her perfect donor."

"A perfect sperm donor?" she asked, her face tense.

John raised his right hand to halt any further query on her part. "Her words, not mine. Valerie asked...well, paid Ambrose a million dollars to help her make that happen. She had the money and that quack Ambrose was more than happy to take a lot of it off her hands."

"I don't understand what any of this has to do with me," she said, more confused than ever.

John rose and went over to the bar and poured himself a drink. Felicia saw a slight tremor of John's right hand as he poured the gold liquid into not one but two glasses. That certainly was an ominous sign. He returned to his desk, placed both in front of him and zeroed in on Felicia's face.

"The donor sperm she used was that of a man she'd been secretly in love with since she was a medical student. The same man her best friend had been in love with—the man who had rejected her in favor of that best friend," he said, never taking his eyes off Felicia.

Felicia felt as though someone had reached a hand into her chest and was squeezing her heart like it was a stress ball. She didn't dare open her mouth to ask any questions. The mere idea that someone...that Valerie, could hurt her in such a way. Felicia still regretted that she'd never allowed her close friendship with Griffin to move beyond the friend zone. That she let fear stop her from pursuing something that she really wanted. Fear of both rejection and acceptance. Felicia knew either reaction would have changed the course she had set for her life. Yet, the idea that the one person who knew what she was prepared to do with and for a love she had yet to experience would betray her in such a way was hard to comprehend, so she remained silent and waited to hear the words.

"The same man, the medical school heartthrob with whom Valerie sabotaged any chance that her friend may have had, was her only option. She couldn't let her friend have something else she couldn't. Valerie made sure that if she couldn't have him, her friend wouldn't have him, either."

Felicia slowly shook her head as a single tear began to fall.

"You were that friend. And I'm so sorry," he said, swallowing hard before adding, "Griffin Kaile…was the donor."

Felicia's mouth fell open and closed just as quickly. The thought that Valerie had sabotaged any potential relationship she could've had with Griffin took root in her mind. She brushed away her tears and reached for the drink John was slowly sliding in her direction. Felicia picked up the glass and tossed the entire contents back in one swallow. She had never been much of a drinker but figured an exception was warranted. Felicia only hoped that the strong, smooth liquid would calm the storm that was building inside her head. She held the empty glass against her lip, feeling the liquor burn its way down her throat.

"Care for another one?" John asked.

"No. Thank you." Felicia placed the glass on the desk. "What I would care for is an explanation."

"You and Valerie may have been friends in medical

school, but she was also very jealous of you," he explained with a hurt look on his face.

"Wh-what?" Felicia stammered.

"Valerie thought everything came easy for you. She told me that you didn't have to work for anything—friends, grades…a man's interest. Valerie said your family's money made you special. That you were only nice to her because you were roommates and you had to be."

Felicia gasped but quickly pressed her lips together, shaking her head like a bobblehead. She was trying to keep the scream she wanted to release from escaping.

"I'm sure your feelings for Valerie were genuine and I have to believe she knew that, as well, at least before she got sick and started making such decisions."

"Such as?" Felicia managed to spit out.

"Valerie paid Ambrose to steal Griffin's sperm, fertilize her eggs and implant them in her uterus," he said.

Anger and disbelief rose to the surface as she gripped the arm of her chair. "How could she do something so vile? To Griffin? To me?" she yelled.

"I'm sorry—"

Felicia held up her right hand, preventing yet another apology from coming forward, which was definitely too little too late and from the wrong person. "While all of this is so ugly, it's also ancient history," she snapped, rising to her feet. "I still don't understand what any of it has to do with me."

John came from around his desk and stood next to her. "Please calm down and let me finish. There's so much more you need to know."

Felicia's hands flew up in surrender as she stepped two feet away from him, moving closer to the door. "I'm sure you do—and this is calm, so cut to the chase. Why am I here?"

"Valerie stole Griffin's sperm and fertilized her egg—"

"Old news. Your point?" Felicia folded her arms, realizing she was channeling her sister Farrah's sharp tongue and being terribly rude, but at this point she didn't care.

"Last January—January fifteenth to be exact—Valerie had a beautiful six-pound baby girl. Griffin's biological daughter. That she wants you to raise as your own."

Chapter 3

Felicia's knees gave way but John caught her before she could hit the floor. He led her back to her seat. Her eyelashes fluttered and taking a breath was not as easy as it should be. Her heart pounded a river of blood through her veins. John reached for his desk phone and hit the call button for his assistant. "Mrs. Ray, get in here quick."

Within seconds the door flew open. An older woman with sienna skin entered immediately and noticed Felicia sliding down in her chair. "Sir, what happened?"

"Help me move her over to the sofa." They each placed an arm under each of her shoulders and walked her over to the sofa. They laid her down and Mrs. Ray placed a pillow under her head.

"Get the first aid kit. There should be some smelling salts in it."

"I don't need that." Felicia waved off the offer as she tried to rise.

"Take your time, my dear," Mrs. Ray warned, handing Felicia a glass of water she'd retrieved for her.

Felicia took several sips as her eyes scanned the two worried faces looking down at her. "My apologies. I think that drink, along with everything else, knocked me off my feet, so to speak." The corners of her lips rose slightly.

"I'm sure it did," John said, returning to the bar and pouring himself another drink.

"Can I get you anything else…should I call someone for you?" Mrs. Ray asked, her wrinkled brow deepening.

"Thank you, but I'll be fine."

"You sure? Because I really don't think you should be driving," she said, her concern clear.

Felicia beamed at the woman's concern. "I have a car service."

"Then, if you need me, I'll be right outside," she said before walking out the door.

"Sorry about all this. I guess whiskey wasn't the best idea, after all," Felicia offered as a form of explanation.

"You sure you're okay?" John asked, leaning against the side of his desk.

"If you're worried I'll faint, I won't. But as far as being okay? Let's see." Felicia tilted her head. "You've just informed me that Valerie, the only woman I've ever been close to other than my sisters, was never *really* my friend. She had a biological child with the man that she knew I had deep, valley-like feelings for, and now she wants me to raise that child as my own." She squished her face and shook her head. "No, I'm far from okay."

John held Felicia's gaze. "You have to understand. After the divorce and finding out that she might not be able to conceive with her own eggs—that her chances were extremely limited—Valerie lost her way a little," John said, tapping the side of his temple with his index finger.

"A little?"

"Okay, a lot," he corrected. "Valerie became obsessed with having a perfect and healthy child by the perfect guy. Again, her words."

"So she decided to steal one, so to speak—Griffin's. Then just give it to me…like it's some type of gift. And why me, especially if she didn't like me as much as you say?" Felicia shook her head in disbelief.

"I think she felt guilty for what she did," he said, breaking eye contact for a brief moment.

"How could she even get away with such a thing?"

"Money...the power it gives. You of all people should know that," he said, and she wasn't sure if that was censure she heard in his tone. "Money can move mountains."

Felicia got to her feet fisting her hands at her sides before slowly pacing around the room. "I think everyone involved in this mess should be arrested and I want that place shut down." Felicia recognized her righteous indignation toward the situation and that her reaction to what Valerie had done was laced with a bit of envy. It wasn't right, but Valerie knew what she wanted and wouldn't let anything or anyone stop her from having it. That was something Felicia only did when it came to her career. She'd never had the courage to go after Griffin and a possible future together when she had the opportunity, and now Valerie had done something she never would; she'd borne Griffin's child.

A lengthy pause ensued, as though he was weighing his response carefully.

"I understand you want some type of retribution and that you're angry—"

"Angry doesn't even come close," she snapped. "And I hope you don't think this is about money. It most certainly won't be once Griffin finds out about all this."

John's eyes grew wide as golf balls. "You're going to tell him?"

"Of course," she said, glaring at John. "He has more rights to Valerie's child than I do."

"He relinquished his rights when he donated his sperm, and notifying Griffin isn't exactly what she wanted. Legally, she's yours," John said, scratching his temple.

Felicia stopped in her tracks. "I don't give a damn what

she wanted and I'm not sure any of this is legal," she said with a heated glare and hands on her hips. "Valerie brought me into this mess and I'll handle things the best way I see fit."

"Of course, but think about the publicity this will bring if what happened gets out," he replied smoothly. "Publicity for everyone involved, including the baby…your daughter."

Felicia's legs almost failed to hold her upon hearing those last two words again; only this time she reached for her chair and sat back down. "My daughter…"

"Yes, your daughter…she needs you." John reached for the folder on his desk, removed a small photograph and handed it to her. "Valerie named her Alyia Blake Kaile Washington."

Felicia accepted the picture without looking.

She took a deep breath and then lowered her gaze. The round face, a light brown color, complete with gray eyes and topped by a head full of black curls, offered a toothless grin that tugged at Felicia's heart. She stared at the beautiful image staring back at her through the photo, a miniature version of her father. The eyes were very familiar. This was Griffin's child.

"Why me?" Felicia asked, keeping her eyes on the photo. "I mean, Valerie had already ruined any opportunity I might have had with Griffin years ago. I still can't believe I let her convince me to stay away from him." *And it didn't take much to convince your scared behind, either.* "Why bring me into this mess now?"

"She felt like she owed you something." John took a seat behind his desk.

"What?" Felicia's eyes widened.

"Let me explain," he said, sounding anxious. "About three months into the pregnancy, Valerie started feeling tired. Actually, too tired. A doctor confirmed that the cancer had returned and this time it had spread."

Felicia's right hand flew to her chest. "Oh, how horrible. She got such news at a time when she should have been celebrating." No matter how angry she might have been at Valerie's betrayal, she knew what she had gone through before, coming to grips and fighting the cancer, and Felicia couldn't help but feel sorry for her.

An injured look spread across John's face. Obviously he'd cared deeply for Valerie. He stood and turned to stare out the window. "Everyone told her that her best option was to terminate the pregnancy. She needed to start fighting for her own life."

"Everyone?"

"Yes. Her doctors…me," he whispered. "But she wouldn't hear of it." The emotion in his voice was almost visible. "All she cared about was having that baby." Each word was laced in sadness.

Felicia tilted her head slightly, peering at him through narrowed eyes. "John, just how close were you and Valerie?"

He remained silent so long that she thought he wasn't going to answer. John's back stayed to Felicia as he stood cracking his knuckles for several moments before his shoulders dropped and he turned to face her. "I loved her, but Valerie never knew it. Our relationship was friendly at best."

"So you never told her how you felt?"

"No. After the divorce, Valerie was determined to start over…on her own. I figured she just needed time, but before I knew it she was pregnant and dying," John explained, and it was clear that he was still grieving his loss.

Felicia's heart sank and her feelings must've showed in her expression because John asked, "Are you okay? Do you need some water or anything?"

"No, I'm fine. Really."

John took his seat behind the extra-wide desk. "Valerie

decided she'd have the baby and fight the cancer after giving birth. She figured she'd beaten it before and she could do it again," he said, shaking his head. "Unfortunately that wouldn't be the case."

"I'm sorry for your loss." Felicia's emotions were taking her on a crazy roller-coaster ride between disbelief, anger and sadness.

John offered a quick nod and continued. "After she gave birth to Alyia, she was told she had less than a year, so Valerie set out to do what she thought was right at the time."

"Which was what exactly?" Felicia frowned and sat straighter in the chair.

John opened his file again, pulled out several documents and handed them to Felicia. She scanned the papers, then she speared John with a look that had him raising his hands in surrender.

"I knew nothing about that until later…much later," he confessed. "I would've tried to convince her to go in another direction, the right direction, much earlier than she did."

Felicia glanced at the paperwork again. "She actually tried to have Griffin's baby adopted. Why?"

"Valerie thought about telling both you and Griffin, so she had you both checked out. But she thought your careers would always come first, that neither of you would ever want the responsibility of a child. She certainly didn't want Alyia to end up alone and in the foster care system… without a family of her own."

The image of the pretty little girl and the possibility of what could happen to her if she ended up in the system sent a chill down Felicia's spin.

"So she figured that while she could, she'd do everything in her power to find her the perfect home."

Felicia stood; she almost went for the whiskey bottle again, an uncharacteristic move for her since she clearly wasn't much of a drinker. Instead she started pacing the room again. "How dare she make such an assumption? I'd never let Alyia end up in foster care. She did all these crazy things just to have Griffin's child and now she was prepared to do yet another crazy thing."

John made his way around his desk and reached out to stop Felicia's progress. "You have to understand what Valerie was going through. She wasn't thinking straight. Her emotions were all over the place."

"No, I don't. I don't have to understand any of this." Felicia could feel her own mixed emotions beginning to boil over to the point she trembled with unspoken rage.

John pulled her into a comforting hug before walking her back to the sofa. "Please sit down. You sure you don't want anything?"

"No," she murmured, wiping away tears with her index finger. "Where is she? Where is Alyia right now?"

"She's being well taken care of, don't worry," John reassured her.

"Don't worry? Are you serious? This child that's suddenly mine…I'm not supposed to worry about?" she asked. "Who's taking care of her?"

"Her nanny, Ellen Lewis. She's been there since the day she was born," he replied. "Alyia's in excellent hands."

"Pardon me if I don't trust Valerie's judgment in selecting caregivers. I assume you have information on this Ellen Lewis. I want to see it," she demanded.

"Yes, of course," he said, returning to his desk and the documents spread across the top. Felicia followed suit and reclaimed her seat. She accepted the documents he handed her and quickly read through them all.

"Looks like she is well qualified," Felicia said, perusing the résumé. "Does she know the truth about all this?"

"She does now. In fact, she insisted that we find you right away."

"Well, that says something," Felicia said, not intending to sound sarcastic, but with the information overload there was no other way to feel.

"That says a lot," he countered. "Ms. Ellen had nothing to do with any of this. She was the wonderful nurse that took care of Alyia when she was at the hospital and Valerie hired her to work in a private capacity. The only reason she accepted was because she thought Valerie was a sick new mother that needed her help."

"Valerie fooled her, too," she snarled, looking up from the documents.

John offered her a tight smile but remained quiet as there was probably no more defense he could offer.

"I've heard enough," she said. "I want to see Alyia. Now!"

Chapter 4

"*Oh...Griffin,*" *Felicia moaned.*

"*You like that, baby?*" *Griffin whispered in Felicia's ear.*

"*Yes, Griffin...oh, yes!*"

Griffin slid his lips along the side of Felicia's neck, stopping long enough to kiss her left shoulder. He raised his head, buried his hands in her hair and captured her mouth in a gluttonous kiss.

"*You've...kept me...waiting,*" *Felicia managed to say between each sensual kiss.*

"*Our wait is over,*" *he declared.*

Suddenly they were both naked and Griffin's tongue exploration of Felicia's body had her reaching for Griffin's engorged and throbbing sex...

The sound of the opening door brought Griffin out of his sexy daydream, a fantasy he couldn't seem to shake, and he was very thankful the newspaper he'd been reading was strategically placed across his lap. It could be a very embarrassing moment for both him and whoever was entering the room.

Mel walked into the lounge. "Dude, you do have an office, you know."

"I know, and everyone knows where it is, too," he replied, keeping his eyes closed.

Mel dropped down in the leather seat across from Griffin. "So you're hiding out in the executive doctors' lounge." He checked his watch. "You've been out of surgery for a couple of hours now."

"Seeing how I'm stretched out in the middle of the room, I'm not exactly hiding, now, am I?" His tone was full of sarcasm.

"Who's a cranky bastard?" Mel said, laughing. "Why don't you just go home?"

Griffin sighed, opened his eyes and glared at his friend. "If you must know, smart-ass, Bishop asked me to take his last two hours of call time. It's his anniversary and he needed to take off early."

"What? Our newly appointed chief—head of the cardiac gods—taking one of his junior doctor's on-call times? No wonder everyone thinks you're some kind of saint." Mel shook his head. "If they could only see how ruthless you are on the basketball court."

"And why are you still here?" Griffin asked, sitting up, planting his feet on the floor. "Your shift ended an hour ago."

"I was chatting up that new, cute, redheaded nurse in Labor and Delivery. We're going out this weekend. What about you? You and your old girl got plans?"

The corner of Griffin's mouth curved upward. "I don't think Jia would appreciate being called old."

"I'm sure, but I wasn't referring to your family's hand-picked girlfriend," he said.

"Then who—?"

"The woman from the airport," Mel said, smiling and nodding.

Griffin rose and went to the refrigerator where he removed a vanilla and strawberry yogurt.

"Hand me one of those juice bottles while you're in there."

Griffin tossed him the drink. "Where are the plastic spoons?" he asked, pulling open drawers.

"Check that box on top of the refrigerator. Come on, man. Spill. What gives?" he asked, cracking the seal of his bottle.

Griffin returned to his spot on the sofa where he sat and stirred his yogurt. "She's...complicated."

"Hell, all women are complicated." Mel took a swig of his drink.

"True, but Felicia's—"

"Wait... Felicia, the one from medical school you told me about? The *if only* woman."

"Yes, that's the one." Griffin tasted his yogurt.

"So what are you going to do?"

"There's nothing to do. She's only in town for the day. I don't even know how to get in touch with her." Griffin ate several more scoops of his yogurt.

"Really?" Mel pulled out his phone. "What's her last name?"

"Blake. Why?" he asked, his eyebrows knitting together.

"I'm looking her up. You know there's this new thing out there called the internet," Mel said, tapping her name into his phone. "You can do some amazing things on it. You should give it a try sometime... Damn, she's a fox and got a lot of awards and commendations, too. Oh, look, there's a number for her company. I bet someone there can get a message to her."

"I'm sure." Griffin tossed his empty container and spoon in the trash. "But did you forget the fact that I told you she works for the government on the other side of the world?"

"And?"

Griffin stood. "I'm going to go round Bishop's patients and then I'm heading out."

"And?" Mel echoed.

"And…me and Felicia? Our time has passed." Between Valerie's warning back in medical school and Felicia blowing him off at the airport, he could take a hint. Griffin walked out the door.

Felicia sat in the back of the limousine with her hands intertwined in her lap. Her whole body was tense and she felt as though her insides were raging and at war. Felicia took a deep breath in an effort to calm herself. They passed several large, immaculately kept homes before turning onto a private street where they traveled an additional few miles before pulling into a circular driveway of what could only be described as a mini mansion.

"Oh, my, what a beautiful home." The two-story, gray-and-white house with large windows screamed elegance.

"Yes, Valerie had excellent taste," John said, the sadness in his voice hard to miss. "There is a five-car garage out back with three cars and a couple of jet skis she takes out on Lake Lanier. Valerie liked her toys." That thought made him smile.

"And this house belongs to Valerie?"

"To you and Alyia now. It's totally up to you to do with as you see fit." John handed her a set of keys. The limo came to a halt as Felicia stared down at the keys.

Within seconds, the door was opened. "Shall we?" John offered his hand.

Felicia gave her head a small shake. "Yes, of course." She exited the limo and walked toward a set of wide, white wooden steps that led to a large porch and a white wooden door.

John reached for the door handle and slowly turned it.

"It's open?" Felicia asked, her eyebrows knitting together.

"I texted Ms. Lewis and asked her to unlock it a few minutes ago. Just as we turned onto the street. I figured you'd need a minute before seeing Alyia."

"Oh… You're right, thanks."

The two entered the house and were greeted by a beautiful foyer with white marble floors as far as she could see. To the left of the entrance was a formal dining room with a twelve-seat, wood and steel table. To the right was a formal living room area with expensive paintings on the walls and contemporary furnishings.

They passed the two rooms and the large marble staircase, into a large open-concept family room. The hardwood floors were covered in beautiful, colored Oriental rugs beneath a half-moon, white-leather sofa with matching chairs. The room was second in beauty to the breathtaking view of the outdoor entertainment area that sat in front of a black-bottomed pool. The place was cold but beautiful, a showcase of wealth with no real signs of life.

"Wow, this place really is something else."

"Wait until you see the rest of it. Upstairs in Alyia's nursery is a sight to behold," John said.

"I'm sure it is, but that can wait," Felicia insisted. "Where is she?"

"I'll go—"

"No need. Here we are," a voice from behind Felicia replied.

Felicia's heart skipped several beats and her breath caught in her throat. She wanted to turn and face the voice but her feet were bolted to the floor.

The other woman must have sensed her trepidation so she came around and faced Felicia. "Miss Blake, I'm so pleased to finally meet you. This is Alyia…your new daughter."

Felicia never even saw the woman's face as her eyes collided with the child she held, a smaller version of a face she hadn't seen in years...not until that morning at the airport. A face with a very unique eye color. Felicia felt drunk with emotion—fear, excitement and a sudden pull toward a child she didn't even know.

"Ms. Lewis, this is Dr. Felicia Blake." John formally introduced them.

John's words broke through the haze of emotion she was feeling. "Hello, Ms. Lewis."

"Please, call me Ellen. Why don't we all have a seat?" she said, moving toward the sofa. "You look like you might fall."

Felicia certainly didn't want a repeat of what had happened in John's office, so she quickly took the seat across from the woman carrying her child. Her child; Felicia still couldn't wrap her head around that thought. John remained standing behind the sofa. Alyia sat on Ms. Ellen's lap, chewing on her plastic rattle.

"Nell, our housekeeper, is upstairs, but she'll be down in a few minutes. Do you want anything to drink?"

"No, thank you," Felicia said, her eyes darting between the woman and the child she held.

"Ms. Lewis, Dr. Blake is—"

"Felicia...please, call me Felicia," she directed both John and Ms. Ellen.

"Felicia has come for her daughter."

"Well, of course she has." She stood and handed a fidgeting Alyia to Felicia.

Felicia's whole body shook as she took Alyia into her arms. The moment Ms. Ellen took a step back, Alyia let out a piercing cry. "You're a doctor, for goodness' sake. You can handle a crying baby," she murmured to herself.

"She's just going to have to get to know you," John offered, giving Felicia a sympathetic smile.

"Yeah, get used to a woman she's never seen in her little life before, who's now in charge of her future. Her new mother." Felicia stated as she continued to try to calm the crying baby. But Alyia twisted her body and cried even louder. Felicia felt like crying herself. This beautiful child, who was now in her care, was rejecting her. She clearly preferred her nanny and that hurt more than Felicia expected. "Why don't you take her for now?" Felicia said to Ms. Ellen as she handed Alyia back to her. She obviously didn't have the same calming touch on Griffin's daughter as she'd once had on him. Felicia's ability to bring Griffin back from frustrating or angry moments was a gift she'd once cherished and only hoped she would master with Alyia.

It was a difficult move to make, in spite of it being the right thing as Alyia stopped crying and clung to the older woman's neck. Felicia was surprised how such a little move made by Alyia, someone she barely knew, a baby at that, could have such an impact on her. Exasperation and helplessness weren't new to the research doctor; the sadness that now accompanied them was.

"If you need time to prepare to take custody—"

"That won't be necessary," she replied to John with a little more bite to her response than she'd expected. Felicia needed her family desperately. She turned to Ms. Ellen, who was now holding a sleepy Alyia over her shoulder. "Are you prepared to continue your role as Alyia's nanny, even if that means leaving Atlanta?"

"Ms. Felicia, I'm a widow with three grown sons who aren't married. So until they decide to give me grandchildren—" she kissed Alyia's cheek "—I'm at this little angel's disposal, no matter where it takes me."

"Good. Please pack your things. We're heading to Texas."

Chapter 5

Felicia exited the limousine, stopping long enough to admire the picturesque lighting display marking the beginning of the holiday season before walking into the lobby of the Mandarin Oriental, one of Atlanta's premier hotels, known for its irresistible Southern charm. Felicia wound her way through its immaculately decorated lobby, when a life-size photo of the only man she'd ever desired stopped her in her tracks…again.

"Griffin," Felicia whispered, staring up at the image.

A beautiful, more confident version of herself came and stood at Felicia's side and looked up at the picture. "Really?" her sister Farrah asked, the sarcasm coming through loud and clear. "I get that Griffin is some big shot now, but is this really necessary?"

"I guess so," Felicia replied, shrugging.

"You okay?"

"I can't believe I'm doing this, and in this dress, too," Felicia said looking down at the sparkly red number that left her shoulders bare and not a single curve to the imagination.

"You returned to Texas nearly a month ago with a beautiful bundle of scrumptiousness in the form of my new niece, determined to do the right thing. Since Dr. Big

Deal—" Farrah used her head to gesture toward Griffin's picture "—refused to reach back out to you after all the attempts you made to contact him, we're forced to return to Atlanta and confront him in person."

"We?"

"Yes, we. You know I wasn't going to let you do this by yourself."

Felicia sighed. "I guess you're right."

"Of course I am. Besides, it's either here or the hospital. And what's wrong with that dress?" Farrah grimaced, causing her brow to rumple.

"I look like you," Felicia replied, her eyebrows standing at attention.

"Of course you do," she said, admiring her reflection in the wall of mirrors leading toward a bank of elevators. "You're one-third of a fabulous set of identical triplets... well, almost identical. What do you expect?"

"I *meant* the dress," Felicia amended on a weary sigh. "This is more your style, not mine."

"I hate to break it to you, baby sister," Farrah said, shaking her head and patting Felicia on the shoulder. "You have no style." Felicia parted her lips to protest but wasn't given the chance as her sister added, "Multicolored scrubs and white lab coats don't count."

In her world, fashion was a distant third to family and focusing on her career, since so many of the diseases she chased could wipe out entire cities within mere days. Felicia glared at her sister, even though she knew she was right.

"That dress looks fabulous on you," Farrah reassured.

"It has all these glittery stones," she said, picking at her dress. "And it's strapless."

"First off, they're Swarovski crystals. And of course the dress is strapless. You have the body to pull it off and it's about time you flaunted it. Besides..." She paused to fix a wayward strand of Felicia's hair and then flashed a look at the poster once again. "You can't see your long-held crush after all these years to tell him that you both have a beautiful nine-month-old baby girl looking anything less than magnificent. You weren't expecting that life-altering news, and neither is he."

Griffin had been Felicia's lab and research partner and close friend since her first day of medical school. While she'd nurtured a secret desire for him, Felicia had always known it would never lead to anything, since he only saw her as a smart, good friend. Besides, they had been headed in different directions professionally, Felicia to the CIA and Griffin to a prestigious cardiac fellowship in Georgia.

"But—"

"No buts. You're a gorgeous woman," her sister said, flipping over a crystal that was turned upside down. "And it's time you showcased it and stopped hiding behind your job. Live a little."

"Like you?" she asked, unable to hide her sarcastic tone while giving her sister's long, black, low-cut halter dress the once-over.

"*Exactly* like me." Farrah smiled, winking at Felicia, showing the more mischievous side that she was known for.

Farrah, the second-born of the Blake triplets, was a no-nonsense corporate attorney for their family's firm. She also didn't believe in filters and considered herself a connoisseur of all things fabulous and expensive. Unfortunately her efforts at getting the most subdued of the three of them to follow in her stiletto-covered footsteps was met with constant resistance.

Farrah grabbed her sister's hand and pulled her forward. "I know why we're here, but how often do you get to dress up for a night out with your big sister?"

"Almost never."

"See, killing two birds with one stone." Farrah offered

her a satisfied grin. "I love how this hotel combined contemporary furnishing and artwork with classic luxury."

"It is lovely," Felicia agreed. "The red roses and calla lily bouquets placed everywhere smell divine."

"Those crystal-drop chandeliers at the front of the hotel," Farrah said, looking over her shoulder, "would look great in our Paris apartment, don't you think?"

"Yes, but focus, please. You sure about this, Farrah?" Felicia frowned, biting her bottom lip. "I mean, we are crashing the man's big night."

"I'm sure, and stop biting your lip," she admonished, frowning and swiping at her sister's hand. "We're not crashing anything. We were *invited* by a client and family friend," she reminded, returning all the smiles and waves being sent their way. "Look, you have to give your boss a final answer about the promotion *and* you have to settle things before you and Alyia make such a big move." She nodded to a man walking past them. "Don't be rude. Loosen up and mingle a little."

Felicia wasn't oblivious to all the attention they were receiving as they made their way through the lobby. In fact, she was used to it. Only, Felicia rarely found herself the center of that attention and never wanted it, for that matter. She was more comfortable being a background singer in their sisterly trio.

"Farrah, wait," Felicia said, halting her progress. "I really don't think this is a good idea. Maybe now isn't the time or the place to spring this kind of news on him."

"Look, sis, we've tried it your way already and you didn't get a response. You've called and left messages, sent emails… Hell, you even sent those damn flowers."

"It was a congratulations gift," she said defensively, breaking eye contact with her sister long enough to ensure she couldn't see through her little white lie.

"Sure…okay. You even included a card that ended with

'Please call me, it's urgent,' and that still didn't get a reaction. So now we do things *my* way and—"

"Dr. Blake…?"

Farrah and Felicia turned toward the sound of Felicia's name.

"Dr. Blake?" a deep voice called out. A tall, handsome man with umber-colored skin, wearing a black Armani tuxedo, approached with an extended hand and a wide smile. "Dr. Felicia Blake, I can't believe it's you. Wow, you're as beautiful as ever." The man's gaze roamed her body before landing on Farrah. "Oh, my, I forgot, there *are* three of you. Well, you're both striking creatures."

Farrah rolled her eyes skyward.

"Dr. David Price," Felicia said, accepting the man's large hand and watching as hers disappeared into his. "This is my sister, Farrah Blake Gold."

"Pleased to meet you," Farrah said, offering a quick nod as she measured up the doctor with a quick once-over.

"Dr. Blake, I haven't seen you since… I don't even know. How long has it been?" Price asked with a seductive grin.

"A little over two years," she replied as her mind brought forward the memory. "We were attending the Boston conference." Felicia turned to her sister and said, "Dr. Price was giving a lecture on cellular microorganisms. He's an expert in the field."

"Sounds…fascinating. Excuse me for a moment." Farrah walked toward a woman wearing a hotel name tag.

"Medicine's not really her thing. She's a lawyer," Felicia explained, wanting to strangle her sister for being so rude.

He laughed. "If I remember correctly, you were living in Texas. What brings you to Atlanta? Are you up for one of those new positions at the CDC? I hear the new executive director came in and cleaned house."

"We're here to visit some old friends," Farrah offered,

making a reappearance. "Please excuse us. We're running late."

"Yes, of course," he said, eyeing both women. He pulled out a business card from the breast pocket of his suit and handed it to Felicia. "Please, give me a call sometime. I'd love to catch up."

Felicia smiled and tucked it away in her crystal-encrusted clutch. "It was nice seeing you again."

"You, too," Price replied as he turned and made his way down the hall.

"The party's right upstairs on the second floor in the Oriental ballroom." Farrah intertwined their arms, pulling her sister toward the escalator, but not before looking over her shoulder at Dr. Price's disappearing form.

"He won't be the only doctor we may encounter," Felicia whispered, trying to slow her sister's pace to no avail.

"True, but there's only *one* doctor here that you need to see. So no distractions allowed."

The sisters took the escalator to the second floor and, with each slow progression, Felicia felt as though the small butterflies in her stomach were growing and if she opened her mouth, they'd make their escape in grand fashion.

"I can't do this," Felicia declared the moment the escalator placed her feet back on solid ground. She gripped her sister's arm and froze, then watched a large crowd of elegantly dressed men and women mill about. She turned and faced her sister, who snatched a glass of wine from a passing waiter. "Farrah, let's get out of here."

"What the hell's wrong with you?" Farrah said before taking a sip of her wine. "You work for the CIA doing God knows what. Dad trained all of us to handle all types of weapons, to fight, and you've even won a few karate matches against both of your sisters, for goodness' sake." Farrah scrunched her face as though her nose had just encountered a vile smell. "Why are you acting like you've never been in a clutch situation before?"

"Oh, I don't know, maybe because all the training in the world hasn't prepared me to tell someone I haven't really seen in years, excluding a ten-minute conversation in an airport weeks ago—a man that I've never so much as shared a real kiss with, a man that I just might still be in love with, which is pretty pathetic if you think about it—that we have a child."

Chapter 6

Felicia spied a ladies' lounge, extracted herself from her sister's hold and weaved through the crowd. She was keeping her head lowered because the last thing she wanted was to be stopped in her current state. Entering the bright room, she spied a small, white sofa and matching round chairs. She took a seat on the sofa and crossed her arms and legs much like a pouting teenager.

Farrah wasn't too far behind. "Really? Is this your plan? Hang out in the ladies' room until the party's over?" she asked, standing with her arms folded, staring down at her sister.

"No, only until the party gets started." Felicia opened her clutch purse, pulled out her cell and checked the time. "It's almost eight. We'll only have to wait another fifteen minutes and then we're out of here. The sooner I get back to the hotel and Alyia, the better."

Felicia decided not to stay at the house Valerie had willed her and Alyia. Considering everything that happened, she felt it would be best if they made a clean break. Felicia decided to put the house up for sale and place the money in trust for Alyia.

Farrah let her arms fall to the sides and joined her sister

on the sofa. "Look, sis, I understand your trepidation for handling things this way, but he's left you no real choice."

"I get that, but I don't think this is the best way," Felicia explained. The door opened and their attention shifted to two ladies making their way past the lounge area and into the stalls positioned behind the sitting room.

Farrah sighed. "All right, so what do you want to do?"

"I want to get the hell out of here and bring Fletcher in to help," she said, her eyes widening and eyebrows rising.

Farrah's eyebrows knit together. "Why Fletcher?"

"He did a great job checking into the attorney who sent me the letter that started this mess in the first place. Fletcher has always found creative ways to resolve our other family problems," she said, giving her sister a smile and a playful nudge. "I'm sure this issue will be no problem. At least for him. He doesn't have any messy emotions to contend with. Fletcher can track him down, break the news, and then the ball will be in his court."

Fletcher Scott, a private detective turned lawyer, was the Blakes' go-to person when it came to handling personal matters the family didn't want their own company involved in.

"Okay, if that's how you want to handle it, so be it." Farrah got up and took a peek outside the door and the sound of live jazz music flowed in. "But by the amount of champagne and the musicians playing in the foyer, we could be here a while. It looks like we'll be missing a great party and you know how I love a good party," Felicia said, returning to her seat where she did a little shimmy.

The sisters laughed, but were interrupted when a pretty, tall woman with features that clearly indicated African-American and Asian heritage, wearing a low-cut, powder-blue, floor-length dress with her hair pulled into a tight bun, entered the lounge area. A petite older woman wearing a more conservative gown in a similar color entered right after. That woman's almond-shaped eyes, high cheek-bones and fair coloring seemed familiar.

Both sisters offered the women a smile. The younger one nodded and stopped at the entrance of the sitting area while the older woman moved forward and extended her hand. "Dr. Felicia Blake," she said, more of a statement than a question. The woman's dark eyes darted between the sisters, clearly confused by the near-identical images before her.

Felicia and Farrah stood, and Felicia accepted the woman's hand. "I'm Dr. Felicia Blake."

"I'm Mrs. Lin Kaile, Dr. Griffin Kaile's mother. We met briefly at Griffin's graduation," she explained, offering Felicia a quick shake with her fingers before dropping her hand as though she was afraid she would catch a disease.

"I remember. Nice to see you again," Felicia replied, suddenly chilled by the woman's icy tone and demeanor. As far as Felicia could remember, there had never been any exchange they'd had that warranted the woman's dismissive behavior.

Mrs. Kaile beckoned the younger woman. "And this is my future daughter-in-law, Jia Richardson." Felicia's heart dropped at the introduction as Jia quickly joined the older woman's side, murmuring something insulting in Mandarin.

Felicia responded to the young woman in the same language, letting them know that she did not appreciate her making such a derogatory statement about her and her sister—that they were like puff pastries, pretty but no substance. She didn't even know them.

Both women turned their glares toward Felicia, who met theirs head-on. Farrah offered her sister a proud smile but remained silent.

Mrs. Kaile broke the silence. "You speak Mandarin?" she asked, leveling an inquisitive stare at Felicia.

"We speak several languages," Felicia replied, smiling at the woman's obvious discomfort.

"I must remember that," Mrs. Kaile responded with a hint of sarcasm in her tone, offering Felicia a tight smile before turning her attention toward Farrah. "Do you speak Mandarin, as well?"

"No, unfortunately I haven't mastered that language yet, but I'm learning. Felicia's an excellent teacher."

Mrs. Kaile's eyes landed on Felicia's face. "You know our language well enough to teach it. I'm impressed," she replied, her face sending a slightly different message, this one of undisguised disapproval.

"If I may ask, why did you say you're not her daughter-in-law *yet*?" Felicia said, putting her focus on Jia.

Before Jia could respond, a trio of women entered the lounge area, but before proceeding any further, they swept a gaze across the others, then made a hasty retreat.

"They're announcing their engagement tonight," Mrs. Kaile clarified. "*After* we celebrate my Griffin's accomplishments, of course. After all, tonight's all about my son."

Butterflies started making their way to Felicia's throat, preparing to make their exit. While the other women may have missed the change in Felicia's demeanor, Farrah clearly did not. "Congratulations. We wish you well," Farrah said, covering for her twin's lapse.

"Yes…congratulations," Felicia managed to force past her lips.

"So you can imagine my surprise when I saw your name on the final guest list, especially since no one in the family invited you," Mrs. Kaile informed her, tightening her grip on the purse she held as if expecting someone to make a grab for it.

Farrah tilted her head slightly. "Yet we *were* invited

and under the impression that this celebration was also a charity event…a fund-raiser for a hospital."

Mrs. Kaile raised her chin slightly. "Yes, of course, Dr. Barry's welcome guest. He's a client of yours, I understand," she said, her lip curving upward slightly.

"He's a family friend," Farrah corrected. "Now, if he were a client, I wouldn't be able to share that information with you. But I'm sure you understand, being the daughter and mother of doctors."

Really, Farrah? Why don't you just tell the woman you investigated every aspect of Griffin's life, including his parents?

The older woman smiled and then dropped it as quickly as it appeared. Her eyes narrowed on Farrah. "You do know quite a bit."

"You have no idea," Farrah said, smiling.

Felicia moved a few inches closer to her sister, saying, "My sister's not only our company's chief legal counsel, she's an excellent investigator," she affirmed. The last thing Felicia wanted was for Farrah to start crossing swords with Griffin's mother and Alyia's grandmother. Especially since they would still have to meet with Griffin at some point and it wouldn't do for there to be bad blood between their families.

"Mother Lin, we should return," Jia said, checking her watch. "It's time to open the doors."

There was a slight pause as the petite woman took in those words. "You're right, my dear. We mustn't keep everyone waiting." Mrs. Kaile gave the sisters a small nod and turned to leave only to turn back to say, "Enjoy yourselves tonight. It's going to be a wonderful evening for Jia and my Griffin."

"Actually—"

"We wouldn't want to be anyplace else tonight," Felicia supplied.

Farrah plastered on a tight smile as she watched both ladies take their leave. They hadn't cleared the area before she whirled to face her sister.

"What changed your mind? I thought you wanted Fletcher to handle things?"

"I do... I did... I mean, I do," Felicia said, frowning.

Farrah laughed. "I think you're right to stay...handle this yourself. Would you want to marry someone without all the facts?"

Felicia dropped down on the sofa, really wishing she could have avoided Griffin's mother and made a faster exit than those women moments before that heated exchange ended. She never understood why Griffin's mother disliked her. "My business is none of hers...not yet, anyway," she declared.

"I'm not talking about *her* and you know it." Farrah stood with her right hand on her hip.

"Oh..." Felicia placed both hands over her face and shook her head.

"Right. Would you want to get married without knowing all the facts that could possibly change your life and perspective on things?"

Felicia lowered her hands. "Wait a minute," she said, rising from her seat and grabbing her sister's arm. "We're not here to stop an engagement. You do get that, right?"

"Of course we're not, but who knows what will result from your little bombshell."

Felicia's right hand flew to her throat and she rapidly shook her head. "No, I can't do this. I won't be the cause of anyone's problem."

"You won't be," Farrah reassured, pulling her sister out of the lounge. "Now let's get going. We have an engagement to stop," she said, laughing as she charged down the hall.

"Farrah Blake Gold, get your butt back here!" Felicia said through gritted teeth, but was talking to nothing but air.

Chapter 7

Griffin stood in the middle of a cozy sitting room, which was only a few doors down from the ballroom where his guests were gathering. The dark wood floors were covered in Oriental rugs and there was a mixture of stylish leather seating. Griffin let the warmth from the floor-to-ceiling fireplace wash over him while enjoying the solitude with a single malt whiskey. This was an important night for him and the hospital, and all he could think about was Felicia and their chance meeting. He often wanted to call her, but her lack of contact spoke volumes. The door flew open and an all-too-familiar voice broke the room's silence.

"There you are, Griffin," his mother said, entering the room then closing the door behind her. "I've been looking everywhere for you."

Griffin turned and offered his mother a wide smile. "Everywhere but here," he said, bending his six-foot frame to kiss his mother on her cheek. "You look lovely, as always."

"Thank you, son. Your father loves me in blue," she said, running her hand across the front of her floor-length, blue lace gown. "He'll let me show off my shoulders but that's about it."

"I know," Griffin said with a laugh then tossed back the

remainder of his drink, placed the glass on a side table and buttoned the jacket of his Kiton tuxedo. "Shall we go?" He offered his mother his arm.

"Not just yet," she said, patting his arm and taking a seat in one of the tall, leather wing-backed chairs. "Sit," she commanded, gesturing toward the matching chair facing hers.

Griffin knew that tone and realized that this wasn't going to be a comfortable little chat. He unbuttoned his jacket, took a seat and leaned forward, resting his forearms on his knees. "All right, Mother, what's going on?"

"Can't a mother just want to talk to her only son, her only child?" she said, offering him a sheepish smile.

"Mother," he said, raising his left eyebrow.

"I thought this might come in handy tonight." She reached into her palm-size purse and pulled out a small, blue velvet box. "This is one of the many rings your father gave me." She placed the box in the center of his hand.

Griffin took in the simplicity of the textured box and then opened it to take in its contents.

"Beautiful, isn't it?" she asked, her eyes sparkling. "Your father has always had great taste. It's a four-carat, flawlessly cut marquise diamond with jade accents. Absolutely perfect for tonight's festivities—a reason to celebrate."

Griffin sat back and sighed. He closed the box and placed it on the small table that sat between them. "Mother, the last time I checked, all my colleagues were here to congratulate *me* on my accomplishments and offer well wishes on this next endeavor." He grimaced. "Not to mention, this *is* a fund-raiser for the hospital."

"Yes, of course," she replied smoothly.

He didn't miss the fact that her gaze darted to the ring box and her own wedding band before reconnecting with his. Griffin's forehead creased. He could always tell when his mother was either up to, or hiding, something, which made her a horrible poker and bridge player.

"But the family is here and so are the Richardsons," she continued. "I just think it would be a wonderful surprise for everyone if you announced your engagement tonight. Right here, in front of everyone," she said with a flourish.

"Mother, I'd be surprised if any one of our family members *wasn't* expecting an engagement tonight. I'm sure you've already prepared them for one."

"Well, you have the ring…"

"Jia and I haven't even discussed marriage," he pressed. "I care for her deeply but it's not…"

The downward turn of his mother's lips was not something he wanted to even try to interrupt. "Never mind." Griffin ran a hand down his face. "Mother, I know you have things all mapped out in your mind, but I have to be honest here. Jia may not be The One."

At that moment a face, memories and even fantasies that plagued his dreams for years suddenly popped into his mind.

Smooth skin. A perfect body he'd craved for far too long. Thought-filled hazel eyes that always seem to call to him and long, black hair that often smelled like vanilla. The way her mind could string a series of chemical and biological facts together that proved her hypothesis so effortlessly signaled that she wasn't like any other woman he'd known.

"Griffin. Griffin, are you listening to me?" his mother asked, her tone rising an octave.

"Yes—no, what was that last bit?"

His mother dropped her shoulders. "The ring, what do you think?"

"The ring is beautiful," he said, turning it over to get a closer look. "Isn't that the fifth one Dad gave you when he proposed? A proposal that you rejected…often, but you still kept the ring?" Griffin asked, laughing more at his father's brilliance at recognizing his mother's manipulation than the fact that she believed she'd been successful at hiding her true sentimental reasons behind rejecting the jewelry he offered.

"Your father was just trying to keep the romantic promise he'd made all those years ago—to get me a proper engagement ring—even though we were already married," she said a little defensively, and each word caused a shock of understanding to whip through him. "Besides, it wasn't exactly what I wanted at the time, but I'm sure Jia would love it. She loves diamonds and jade, and it's big and expensive. It speaks to our station," she proudly expressed.

"And that's what this marriage is all about. It's for you, isn't it, Mother?"

Griffin stood and walked toward the fireplace, taking in its crackling while trying to keep his composure. While he loved his mother, her constant interference could wear on him. She had been the one who had pushed until he began to date Jia. She thought their similar heritages, her elevated financial status and Jia's submissive upbringing made her his perfect match.

Griffin turned back and faced his mother. "You think she'd be a good fit for me, regardless of what we feel for each other. What about love and passion?"

While he knew it was ridiculous, Griffin couldn't help but think that, if given the chance, he and Felicia could be happy. That she could even meet his mother's high standards.

His mother waved off his concerns with a delicate hand. "Don't be ridiculous. You're much smarter than that. Marriage is a partnership, and you have a marvelous future ahead of you. You need an appropriate wife by your side. Love and passion are irrelevant, but they will come."

"You adore Father. You fought your family to be with him," he reminded her, slipping into Mandarin.

"Yes, I do…and I did. I lost my family in the process, too," she replied in Mandarin before switching back to English. "While that will never be your worry, son, I do want what's best for you. I know your father would agree that a partner that wants the same things as you is worth her weight in silver, gold and uncut diamonds." She laughed, placing a hand over her heart. "I love it when he tells me that."

At that moment the door opened. "I thought the party was down the hall," a deep baritone voice coming from an older, gray-eyed version of his son, wearing a similar black tux, said. He crossed the threshold and made his way to his wife's side. "Everything is ready and they've started to let everyone in. You two plan on joining us anytime soon?"

"Hello, Father." Griffin hugged the only man he ever admired as if he was the life preserver he so desperately needed.

"Of course we are," Lin said, greeting her husband with a quick kiss on his bearded cheek. "I'm just trying to convince your extremely stubborn son that tonight would be the perfect time to propose to Jia."

Griffin's gaze met his father's in the hope that he could read him like always. "Oh, Lin, let the boy be. He'll make his choice in his own time."

Lin turned her attention to her husband, eyes flashing with a silent warning. "The time is now and you know it! Between his new position at the hospital and his commitments to the company, he's going to need a strong, uncomplicated partner by his side. Not to mention she's beautiful, sharp as a sword, comes from a good family and can't wait to have children."

"But, dear—"

"No buts." She turned her attention back to Griffin.

"Look, darling, we only want what's best for you." She glanced over her shoulder at her husband, a move she often did when she was expecting his full agreement, which she got with a smile and a nod. Lin's smile surpassed that of her husband as her gaze zoomed in on her son, who wasn't smiling at all. "Just think about it, darling."

Griffin knew his mother meant well and she may have even been a little right. However, he also knew that what he felt for Jia wasn't what he'd once felt for the woman that got away. Griffin certainly wasn't sure he was ready to settle for anything or anyone less.

"I'll think about it, Mother, but I'm not making any promises."

Lin smirked, captured her husband's hand and led him to the door. "Take a minute, but you have a ton of folks waiting to hear from Grady Memorial's new cardiac chief."

Griffin Sr. smiled. "We're very proud of you, son."

"Thanks, Father." He watched as his parents walked out the door.

Griffin's heart expanded every time his father used those words. He buttoned his jacket and headed for the exit just as he heard a small knock before the door slowly opened. He stopped short at the sight standing before him. Griffin's breath caught in his throat and he thought he might be going into shock. Had his nostalgic moments conjured a beautiful illusion?

"Felicia… Felicia Blake?" he whispered to the woman standing in the doorway and then frowned when a vibe that hit him said the name didn't quite fit. "Wait…you're not Felicia."

"Very good," the woman said, taking a step back. Someone else, someone identical in almost every way, came and took her place.

"Hello, Griffin," Felicia said barely above a whisper.

Chapter 8

Felicia slowly crossed the room's threshold, and just the sight of Griffin with his thinly trimmed beard and those beautiful gray eyes was enough to resurrect the butterflies she thought she had under control. She tried to stay calm and open her mouth to add a memorable follow-up to her greeting, only to have her inner geek take over.

"Congratulations on your new assignment. Head of the Grady Cardiac wing. Quite impressive. I understand that Dr. West and Dr. Baker were both contenders for the position," she said, trying to ignore the way he was looking at her—like she'd just hit him with a Taser.

Griffin continued to stare in silence.

"However, your clinical accomplishments in the field outweigh Dr. West's research on animals. Not that clinical research isn't important, especially to someone like me, but that can't hold a candle to actual human successes. As for Dr. Baker—"

"As fascinating as I'm sure all this may be…" Farrah said, glaring at her sister.

Real smooth, Felicia.

"I'm Farrah, Felicia's older sister. The lawyer." Farrah offered her hand.

Griffin accepted her hand and gave it a shake. "Yes, of

course. I remember you had a couple of sisters…triplets," he said to Felicia, who smiled. "Pleased to meet you, Farrah."

Farrah went to take a seat on one of the small chairs facing the couple.

"What are you doing here?" His confused look was almost charming. "Excuse my shock, but when I didn't hear from you I thought… Never mind what I thought. I don't recall seeing your name on the invite or the RSVP list," he explained.

"It was a last-minute decision. We're in town to handle some family business and when Tim Barry invited us to be his guest to celebrate your new assignment…well, I couldn't say no," Felicia explained, hoping she wasn't as red as she felt. Thankfully her brain had kicked back into gear and she was able to bring forward the story she and Farrah had finally come up with. One that didn't have her simply blurting out the truth as Farrah would have preferred: ripping the baby bandage right off, so to speak.

"Well, I'm pleased you didn't." Griffin took Felicia's left hand and slowly brought it up to his lips while never taking his exotic eyes off hers. He kissed it gently. "It's wonderful to see you again. You look absolutely—"

"Different," she said, glancing downward at the dress Farrah had talked her into. "Not quite how you're used to seeing me."

"Oh, brother, you can't even take a compliment," Felicia heard her sister murmur.

Griffin laughed. "No, but what I was going to say is that you look absolutely beautiful. Although I've always thought you were stunning." Their eyes collided and an electric current passed between them.

Felicia quickly pulled her hands free. "Thank you. You're looking pretty handsome yourself."

Farrah cleared her throat. "Now that the pleasantries

are out of the way," she offered, clearly giving Felicia the opening she needed.

Felicia was starting to regret her sister's interference and the offer she'd originally made to join her on this excursion.

"Yes, please allow me to show you to your table." Griffin reached for Felicia's hand again, gifting her with a sexy smile, and squeezing it slightly, a move that erased every thought from her mind at that moment. "Maybe later, after I'm done with all the speeches and whatnot, we can meet for a drink…catch up on things. Are you staying at the hotel?" His eyes widened slightly and his tone rose an octave.

The untapped woman inside the brilliant, closed-off doctor was ready to accept when she noticed the ring box he still held in his left hand; all of those pleasant feelings came to a complete halt. It was like being hit in the face with a bucket of ice water. Felicia extracted her hand and took a step back. Griffin's nearness and whatever siren-calling cologne he wore were making her dizzy.

"That would be great," she admitted. *If you weren't about to get engaged.* "But the truth is, I've been trying to reach you about an urgent matter that we need to discuss. When we heard and saw your father leave you alone, I figured now was the time, especially since my calls and emails—"

"And flowers, let's not forget those damn flowers," Farrah added, garnering an angry glare from Felicia—one she ignored. Clearly, Farrah was enjoying how things were starting to unfold; she tapped her index finger on her clutch as a reminder that she had the necessary paperwork and was prepared to take over if need be.

Griffin's glare bounced between the sisters. "What calls? What emails? I certainly never saw any flowers you might have sent."

"Not *might*. Did send," Farrah stressed and her irritation didn't go unnoticed by Griffin, who frowned.

"My apologies. Did send," he amended. "However, I never received anything from you, Felicia." Griffin's eyes hardened and his smile disappeared. "I would've called you back. In fact…" he stated, breaking eye contact.

"In fact what?" Felicia asked barely above a whisper.

"I've often wondered how you were, where you were at any given time. I've followed your career…your accomplishments. I know you work for our government," he explained, his smile returning as he put the ring box in his jacket pocket.

Felicia's heart flipped until the next words fell from his beautiful lips. "A research scientist for the CIA…impressive. That must be very fascinating and fulfilling work. I'd love to hear more about it sometime. That is, if you don't have to kill me," he said, offering up a small laugh.

Her heart sank. It was just like old times. Griffin was more interested in the work and not her. *Get a grip, girl. The man's about to get engaged. Skip to the point.*

"That would be nice, and at some point I'm sure we'll catch up on our work. However, the reason I've been trying to reach you is of a more personal nature."

"All the more reason we should find time to meet later tonight," he insisted. "So…are you? Staying here at the hotel?"

"No, we're staying at the Four Seasons, but—"

"That's great." Griffin checked his watch. "I better get out there before my mother sends out the National Guard, and that's not an exaggeration. Their chief is an invited guest. Let's meet in their main bar…say, ten thirty?"

"Well…" Felicia bit her bottom lip and glanced over at her sister.

"Great. What's the topic of this important personal discussion, anyway?" Griffin asked, moving toward the door and adjusting his pocket handkerchief.

Felicia looked over at Farrah, who offered her a supportive nod. She turned back to Griffin. "Alyia Blake Kaile Washington, your daughter. Our daughter, actually."

Griffin froze and flinched under the power of those words. A shadow of disbelief and shock flittered across his face.

So much for not ripping the bandage off.

Griffin slowly turned to face Felicia, knowing he must have misunderstood the last words that slipped from her beautifully inviting lips. As many times that he'd dreamed about taking Felicia to bed, he most certainly would have remembered if he actually had.

"Run that by me one more time."

"Alyia Blake Kaile Washington," she said. "Our daughter. Let me explain."

All this time he had envisioned her to be brilliant, strong and adventurous; not once did it cross his mind that she was mentally imbalanced.

"Felicia, we both know that's not possible." Griffin's voice had taken on a harsh tone that had Farrah sitting up in her seat.

"Actually…" Farrah started to explain when both Griffin and Felicia shot her a look that clearly meant she should stop speaking.

"I'll handle this," Felicia stated, holding up her right hand.

"Yes, someone handle it." Griffin stood staring down at Felicia.

A more subdued Felicia matched Griffin's stance. "Look, Griffin, I realize this comes as a shock."

"Shock! Not even close. It's *impossible*." Griffin shoved his hands in his pockets to keep from reaching out and either strangling Felicia for coming to try to run some type of game on him, tonight of all nights, or kissing her senseless because he still wanted her so damn bad.

"It's not, actually."

"Yes, it is. You and I have never had sex of any kind… *ever.*"

Felicia's eyes drifted downward and she slowly shook her head. Griffin thought he'd cleared whatever fog she was dealing with or simply stopped her game in its tracks. "Now, this has been…interesting, but I have an event to attend. Under the circumstances, I think it would be best if you didn't stay. Of course, I can't make you leave, but I'd appreciate it—"

"Wait just one damn minute," Farrah demanded, coming to stand near them.

Felicia tightened her grip. "I got this, Farrah."

"Then get it before I do."

What's with these two? "Look, I'm not sure what you two are after or if you're just delusional, Felicia, but I don't have time for this foolishness."

"Delusional? My sister is a brilliant physician," Farrah declared, her tone hard and hostile.

"I know a lot of brilliant but delusional physicians," Griffin countered, giving her glare measure for measure.

Felicia gifted Griffin with a smile that didn't quite reach her eyes. He noticed Felicia using her free hand to squeeze her sister's forearm. "I'm not after anything, Griffin. And I'm sure you do think I'm crazy, but I promise you that I'm not. If you let me explain, you'd understand. However, there is one thing that I do need."

Griffin's shoulders dropped and his expression shifted from annoyance to mocking. "Here we go. How much?"

"Money? You think she's after your *money*?" Farrah bellowed. "So much for you keeping up with her life. Besides working for the CIA, you do realize she's an heir to our family's multi*billion*-dollar company, right?" She waved her hand in a dismissive gesture. "You might want to look us up."

"Farrah," Felicia admonished.

"Then what is it that you need?" he asked, his arms folded across his wide chest.

Felicia raised her chin, meeting his glare. "Your medical history. For Alyia—"

"Not that again," Griffin grumbled. "How far are you going to take this?"

Felicia heaved a sigh and dropped her sister's arm. "Give it to him," she told Farrah.

Farrah reached into her long, crystal-covered purse and pulled out a white envelope and a business card. "Here's the letter from Valerie Washington's attorney, along with a copy of the DNA results, as well as my card. As Felicia explained earlier, I'm not only her sister, I'm her attorney. Have yours call me…soon!"

Griffin's eyes widened slightly, a move that Felicia hadn't missed. "Valerie Washington…what does she have to do with any of this?"

"Read the letter. It explains everything," Felicia said, her voice barely above a whisper. "Well, enough of it, anyway."

Griffin accepted the card and envelope from Farrah while keeping his eyes on Felicia. The lone tear that fell from her beautiful face told him that somehow she *actually* believed this ridiculous story was true. Not only was Griffin sure that he and Felicia had never had sex, he was just as sure he'd never touched Valerie Washington…

They seemed harmless enough, but maybe he should be calling security to remove them from the premises.

Farrah grabbed Felicia's hand and pulled her toward the door.

Felicia stopped long enough to say, "Sorry about all of

this. I know the timing sucks. Congratulations on your engagement. I wish you nothing but the best."

"My engagement?" Griffin's hand flew to the pocket of his jacket. Before he could respond, the sisters were through the door, down the hall and heading for the exit. Griffin stood in the doorway and watched their retreat.

What the hell just happened?

Chapter 9

"There you are," Griffin heard Jia call from behind.

He turned to face her, his expression tight. "Your parents are freaking out. Everyone's asking for you and it's almost time for your speech."

"Yes, of course," he said, glancing down at the envelope and card he still held.

"What's that?" Jia asked, offering up a megawatt smile.

Griffin quickly folded the envelope and placed it and the card in the inside pocket of his jacket. "Nothing that can't wait."

"You sure?" she asked, straightening his tie. "You look upset. Did something happen?"

"Nothing I want to talk about right now, anyway." He planted a quick kiss on her cheek, a move that suddenly didn't feel right. Griffin took Jia by the elbow and guided her toward the ballroom but not before glancing over his shoulder in the direction Felicia had vanished.

Jia stopped Griffin before they made it to the ballroom doors. "Look, I don't want you to do anything tonight or ever, until you're absolutely ready." Jia smoothed out the lapels on his jacket. "I know your mother is only doing what she thinks is best. However, this is our life and we have to do what's best for us and the family I hope to share with you one day."

Griffin's hand seemed to move to his pocket on its own accord and he smiled. "I appreciate you saying that, but I know exactly what I have to do. We'll talk after my speech."

Jia's face lit up with excitement and she gave a breathy, "Of course."

Griffin knew that if what Felicia claimed was even remotely possible, his life would change completely.

How much was yet to be determined.

Felicia slid the black security key card down the door's lock for the third time, only to be hit with another blinking red light. "Dammit!"

"Just knock. Ms. Ellen will let us in," Farrah said, leaning against the wall in the small circular foyer.

"I don't want to wake Alyia. And, besides, where's your key?" she said, sliding the card again to no avail.

"I left it on the dresser. May I?" Farrah asked, reaching for the card.

"Fine!" Felicia huffed, releasing a frustrated sigh but complying all the same.

Farrah took the card, swiped it and smiled when the green light appeared. She opened the door and stood aside to let her sister enter. "The younger, more irritated sister..." she began in a taunting tone that matched one of a news reporter. Then she waved her hand, gesturing Felicia forward. "Before the wonderful sister," Farrah added, laughing, walking over the threshold, sidestepping her sister's playful nudge.

Felicia moved through the living room and down the hall to a large, corner-bedroom suite. She slowly opened the door to a dimly lit room to find Ms. Ellen slowly rocking Alyia in a glider rocker, her eyes closed, humming a tune she didn't recognize.

"Ms. Ellen," she whispered, noticing the smell of baby powder throughout the room.

Ms. Ellen opened her eyes but continued to hum as she smiled. "You're home early," the dark-eyed, gray-haired beauty said, continuing to stroke the back of her young charge.

"Things didn't go exactly as planned." Felicia took a seat in a small chair across from the glider. "Has she been sleeping long?"

"Not at all. Care to take her?" she asked, leaning forward.

"No… I mean, I don't want to disturb her. I guess I just wanted to check on her."

"Of course you did," Ms. Ellen said, smiling. "She's your daughter."

"I guess I'm still trying to get used to the fact that I even *have* a daughter. Well, at least she will be."

"Honey, you know she's already yours. All you have to do is look in her face whenever you're near her. The way her eyes light up…how she smiles and reaches for you. She's your daughter. You may not have given birth to her, but she's definitely your child. Even her eyes are similar to yours."

The corner of Felicia's lips rose slightly. "Actually, those came from her father, although his are lighter."

"I bet they're lovely."

"Yes, they are," Felicia said, dropping her smile, remembering the hard glint in them when she'd left him tonight.

"You sure you don't want to hold her before I put her down?" Ms. Ellen asked, brushing her hand across Alyia's hair.

"No. I think I'll just go get out of this ridiculous outfit and get ready to call it a night." Felicia stood and smoothed out her dress. "Do you have everything you need?" she inquired, glancing around the room full of stuffed animals and the soft toys littering the floor between the daybed-style crib and Ms. Ellen's queen-size bed. There was more than enough entertainment to keep a nine-month-old busy.

"Oh, yes, my dear. I'll put this little one down and watch one of my movies on that nice iPad you gave me, before calling it a night myself."

"Well, thanks again. For everything. I really don't think I could've handled this adjustment alone."

She smiled. "Child, you're not alone. Between your family and me, you're already several steps ahead of the game. The way you've handled this whole thing has been commendable."

Felicia offered the older woman a tight smile before reaching down and kissing Alyia on the crown of her head. "Good night."

Felicia made her way across the hall to her own bedroom suite, which was illuminated by the lights of the city as the floor-to-ceiling drapes had been left open. The big inviting king-size bed had been turned down and the hotel's complimentary bathrobe was placed across the bottom of the bed. Felicia tossed her purse on the bed and went to stand in front of the window. "Commendable…right."

Felicia couldn't think of one commendable thing about this whole mess, especially how she'd handled things with Griffin.

After seeing a disappointed Jia back to her place after the party, Griffin made his way home. He sat back in his favorite chair in front of his bedroom's fireplace, nursing a glass of twenty-year-old single-malt Scotch whiskey. He hated hurting Jia, but even before Felicia's visit, Griffin knew he couldn't marry her.

Griffin knew he should feel a sense of accomplishment…joy, even, but that was the furthest thing from his mind. He had done what he'd set out to do—raise two million dollars for the hospital's children's cardiac wing. Unfortunately the only thing he'd been able to think about was Felicia and what had now turned out to be her much-founded charges.

Griffin reread the one line in the DNA report that stood out and would change his life forever. "'There is a 99.9% certainty that donor G00088987K, aka Griffin Kaile Jr., is the biological father of baby girl Alyia Blake Kaile Washington,'" he read out loud. It was as if hearing himself speak the words would make the reality of the situation sink in. The fact that Valerie explained how she used Griffin's sperm donation to confirm paternity didn't make this news any easier to swallow. Griffin took another sip of his drink before allowing his mind to travel back to the day he'd made a decision that was now taking a different and unexpected direction.

"I think this is a lovely thing that you and your friends are doing. Not many young people would make such a wonderful sacrifice," the older nurse explained.

"Thank you, Nurse Tina," Griffin replied, reading her name tag. "We're doctors in training. We know how important it is to help people in need and to look out for our futures. Cancer can destroy the body, but it doesn't have to destroy one's spirit. If you can offer a solution, I think you should. That's all we're doing." Griffin made his passion clear.

"That's very noble," she said on a small laugh. "Although a couple of your friends are here for the money. They make donations a lot."

Griffin smirked and shook her head. "I'm not surprised."

"Well, Mr. Kaile. All of your paperwork seems to be in

order," Nurse Tina said, closing the file and reaching for a specimen kit. "You ready?"

"Yes, ma'am."

"Room C is available." Tina walked him to the door. "There are magazines and movies in there if you need help," she explained.

"Thank you. I'm sure I'll figure it out." Griffin walked into the room and closed the door.

Griffin took a deep breath, releasing it slowly before taking another sip of his drink. He pushed the past out of his mind and shook his head. Griffin pulled out his phone and dialed his friend and personal lawyer, Cooper Johnson, for some much needed advice.

"Griffin, do you know what time it is?" Cooper asked.

"It's time for you to start earning that big fat retainer of yours," Griffin responded.

Cooper laughed. "Dude, didn't I just leave you at your event where I also gave *you* a big fat check?"

"Are you sober? Because I need some advice."

"Of course. What's going on?" Cooper's tone instantly turned serious.

"You're not going to believe this." Griffin spent the next forty-five minutes bringing Cooper up to speed on everything he knew about what Valerie had done and Felicia's role as he understood it so far.

"I'll swing by your place in the morning and pick up a copy of the letter and report, but if all this is true, you should be on solid legal ground with whatever you decide to do," Cooper assured him confidently. "Everything I told you when you explained what you did back in the day still stands. I have all your original paperwork from that decision with your will."

"Thanks."

"Should I even try and convince you to stay away from

Felicia until you hear back from me? You are paying me a big fat retainer for this advice," Cooper said sarcastically.

"I'll see you tomorrow." Griffin ended the call.

Looks like Felicia and I will have a future together after all. Too bad it's not in the way I hoped. "Damn you, Valerie. How could you do such a thing?"

Chapter 10

"Felicia," Farrah called out as she entered her sister's bedroom, drying her hair with a thick, thirsty towel. She had changed into a pair of white leggings and a long, white T-shirt. Felicia's glassy eyes met her sister's gaze and offered her a small, tight smile.

"Honey, you okay?"

When no answer was forthcoming, Farrah tossed her towel across the bed, allowing her long hair to hang down her back as she made her way across the room.

"No. No, I'm not," she cried, throwing herself into her sister's arms.

"Oh, Felicia," she whispered, walking her sister to her bed where they both sat in silence for several minutes. "You're not still upset about Griffin, are you?"

"Maybe," she murmured then nodded, her head now resting on her sister's shoulders. "This whole thing is a mess and Alyia's caught in the middle of it."

"Baby sis, it really isn't, and my beautiful niece is just fine. Griffin will come around, share his medical history and sign off on you having sole custody, just like you want. He doesn't have the time or the desire for a baby, especially an unplanned, basically stolen baby, at that. He did donate his sperm, after all. Anyway, he has what's-her-name whenever he is ready for a family."

Felicia sat up and took a deep breath. She wiped away her tears with the back of her hand. "I hope you're right. Although—"

"No, you don't. You tried the nice approach and he shut you down."

"Come on, Farrah. Griffin has every right to be shocked. Hell, *I'm* still in shock and I've had a few weeks to deal with it."

"Shocked, not rude." Farrah reached over and switched on the light sitting on the nightstand. "That's better. Look, I know you still have a thing for Griffin, and deep down in that ungrazed and inexperienced heart of yours, you're hoping things might work out somehow between you two."

Felicia sat straighter. "Don't be ridiculous. This isn't about some schoolgirl crush I had a million years ago. We're talking about a child."

"Yes, one we're both pretty sure he won't want," Farrah declared.

"You don't know that, and it's not fair to make that assumption based on a knee-jerk reaction," Felicia acknowledged, pulling some of her clothes from the dresser drawer.

Farrah lay across her sister's bed, resting her face on her left hand. "Whatever you say, sugarplum princess. Let's just wait for his response or the response from his attorney, which is more likely."

Felicia shook her head. "I'm going to go take a shower so I can get in the bed. Alyia will be up before you know it."

Farrah flicked a glance at a digital clock. "It's not even ten yet. Besides, Ms. Ellen will have Alyia."

"How can I learn to be her mother if I'm not watching and learning how to take care of her? Most women have nine months to prepare, but I didn't get to do any of that.

In all those books I've read about becoming a mother to an adoptive child, my so-called maternal instincts should have fully kicked in by now, but they haven't yet."

"What are you talking about? You're great with Alyia." Farrah ran her hand through her hair. "And Ms. Ellen's got your back. She's doing a great job. At least Valerie did something right."

"I know, but I'm her mother. At least I'm trying to be," she whispered. "By the way, don't you have a husband to call?"

"What do you think I was doing before I came to check on you?"

"Showering." Her eyes zeroed in on Farrah's damp hair.

Farrah presented her sister with a wicked smile and made her eyebrows dance. "Why do you think I needed a shower after talking to my sexy husband?" she said, laughing so hard that she almost rolled onto the floor.

"Get your crazy, still-wet-hair-having butt off my bed," Felicia demanded, trying but failing to hide her amusement. "And go to your room."

Farrah stood. "Don't hate. Seriously, are you going to be all right?"

"I'm fine. It's just been an emotional day."

Farrah kissed her sister on the cheek. "Well, I'm here if you need me. Night-night."

"Night."

Felicia woke to the smell of fresh roasted coffee wafting through the suite and the animated sounds of a Saturday morning cartoon coming from a television. She pulled herself out of bed, gathered up her things and headed to the bathroom. *Me still having a thing for Griffin after everything that's happened...don't be ridiculous. So what if I am having nightly sex dreams about Griffin and fantasiz-*

ing about us having a family together? That's hormones and circumstance.

Felicia showered, pulled her hair into a high ponytail and wrapped her body in her silk robe. She made it to the living room, where she spotted her sister sitting at the dining room table eating pancakes and eggs as she read the *USA TODAY* newspaper. Ms. Ellen was feeding a smiling Alyia, who was sitting in a high chair, oatmeal smeared around the edges of her mouth.

"Good morning, everyone," Felicia said, pouring herself a big cup of coffee. She added two drops of cream before taking a seat next to Alyia. Their eyes met and Alyia started jumping in her chair and laughing. Felicia reached over and gave her a quick kiss on her forehead, taking in the sweet smell of her shampoo. "How did she sleep?" she asked Ms. Ellen.

"Like an angel, as usual. She woke up at eight on the dot. Like a clock, this one," Ms. Ellen responded, brushing several long curls from Alyia's face.

"Felicia, that child needs a haircut bad," Farrah offered, putting her newspaper aside.

"No, she doesn't," Felicia said, brushing her hand through Alyia's hair, removing it from her face. Alyia bent her head to the side and smiled as though welcoming her mother's touch.

They all laughed.

Farrah's eyes swerved from Felicia to Alyia. "I can't get over how much she seems to look like you, even though you didn't actually give birth to her."

Felicia smiled at her sister. "It's all those dark curls." She turned her attention to her daughter. "Are you done, my beautiful, messy girl?"

Alyia threw her hands up and giggled, a clear indication that she wanted to be picked up. Felicia laughed, pulled out a wet wipe from the disposable package that sat on the bar and quickly wiped Alyia's face. Alyia shook her head, sending black curls flying everywhere.

Felicia freed Alyia from her high chair, held her close, inhaling her skin's baby-powder-sweet smell before kissing her cheeks. "Such a sweet girl," she murmured as she stood slowing rocking her in her arms. She adored her baby and was going to do everything in her power to keep her safe and happy.

Maybe those instincts have kicked in, after all.

"I'll go clean this little one up and put on that cute little pink-and-yellow-flowered dress for the trip to the museum, if you don't mind," Ms. Ellen said, reaching for Alyia.

"Not at all." Felicia reluctantly handed over her baby.

"Well, I better go get dressed myself. I have a quick meeting before we head back to Texas."

Farrah stood, tossed her napkin over her empty plate and picked up her newspaper. She had nearly caught up with Ms. Ellen when she stopped, looked over her shoulder and said, "I ordered you some breakfast a few minutes ago. They should—" There was a knock on the door. "Right on time," Farrah said, continuing on to her bedroom.

Felicia grabbed a pen from the bar so she could sign for her breakfast and opened the door. "Good—"

"Good morning to you, too," a baritone voice replied, its bearer smiling down at a wide-eyed Felicia who was using the door to keep herself upright. "We need to talk," Griffin said, sending familiar waves of desire through Felicia's body.

Felicia had to blink a couple of times to make sure she wasn't dreaming. Lord knows how many ways the man standing before her draped in a gray Givenchy suit had appeared in her erotic dreams last night.

Chapter 11

"Can I come in?" Griffin asked, standing with his hands in the pockets of his expertly tailored pants. His eyes swept over Felicia's body. Griffin's mouth curved up when Felicia tightened her robe, trying to hide her erect nipples, which were pressing against the silk robe.

"What are you doing here?" she asked with a slight frown.

"I told you, we need to talk. You drop a bombshell on me and you think that's it? That I'd just let my attorney handle it?" he asked, trying to control his anger and the sudden flash of desire for the woman standing before him. "Can I come in?"

"Yes, of course." Felicia stepped aside, allowing him access.

Griffin crossed the threshold and entered the living room. His eyes scanned the room, landing on the empty high chair next to the table littered with dirty dishes. He angled to face Felicia. "Is the child here?" he asked, his tone slightly hard.

"Yes, *she's* here," Felicia said with a disapproving set to her jaw.

There was a knock on the door. "Expecting company?"

he asked, and for some reason the words held a possessive edge he couldn't explain.

"Not that that's any of *your* business, but I'm sure that's my breakfast," she said, moving past him to get to the door. Felicia signed the invoice and accepted the tray before turning her attention to Griffin. "Look—"

"Don't let me stop you. Please, eat. I can wait." Griffin took a seat on the sofa and focused on the woman in front of him. He had always thought Felicia was exquisite, but this fresh-faced, confident, barefoot woman was a vision and wreaking havoc on his senses.

"I don't think—"

Farrah entered the room adjusting her earrings. She'd changed into a gray pantsuit and her hair was pulled back into a tight bun. "Look, sis, if Griffin…" Farrah dropped her hands and stopped speaking at the sight of the man rising from his seat. "Well, well, look what the dog dug up," she said, placing her right hand on her hip.

"Farrah, please," Felicia admonished, standing with her hands in her robe pockets.

"Ms. Blake," Griffin greeted.

"Mrs. Gold, actually. I expected to hear from your attorney. What are you doing here?"

What am I doing here? Is she serious? "I thought your sister and I should talk. Without attorneys being involved. No offense." He raised his right hand.

"Well, offense taken."

"Farrah, please…"

"We're all set for our trip to the children's museum," Ms. Ellen announced as she entered the room with a smiling Alyia who was holding a rattling toy.

Griffin's eyes zeroed in on the child. He felt like he'd just been hit in the chest.

"Excuse me, I didn't realize someone was here." Ms.

Ellen handed Felicia her phone. "It was playing that special work ringtone, so I thought you might need it."

The air in the room seemed to have been sucked out and Griffin was sure his face had lost some of its coloring. He watched as the happy child with eyes exactly like his own made her long black curls dance. She was bending her body from side to side, squirming in the woman's arms. She clearly didn't want to be held any longer. Griffin felt himself being pulled forward and he took a step toward the child, a move that didn't go unnoticed.

Farrah matched Griffin's steps. "Ms. Ellen, can you take—"

"No," Felicia said, taking her eyes off her text message. "It's all right, Farrah. Ms. Ellen, we need to delay our trip a bit. I'm still not even dressed and we've had a surprise visitor. Ms. Ellen, this is Griffin Kaile. Alyia's father," Felicia introduced.

"Pleased to meet you," she replied, giving him a wan smile.

"And you…too. I mean, I'm pleased to meet you, as well," he clarified, shaking his head.

Ms. Ellen offered a small nod in return. "Why don't I just put Baby Girl down in her playpen for a while?" she offered.

"Great idea." Felicia turned to Griffin. "Please have a seat. You and Ms. Ellen can keep an eye on Alyia while I change and deal with this call."

"Sure," Griffin said, finally finding his voice and losing a little of his heart to his daughter. "No problem."

Watching Griffin and Alyia together made her heart expand. *Maybe we can… Stop it. He's here about Alyia. Just stay in the moment. Let's just find out what he wants.* "Farrah, can I speak to you for a moment?" Felicia pulled Farrah down the hall and into her bedroom before she could answer. "Look, I know you mean well, but I've got everything under control."

"Sure you do," Farrah said, standing with her weight on her right leg and her hands on her hips.

Felicia went to her closet and snatched out a multicolored scoop-necked shirt and a pair of tattered jeans. "This is something I think Griffin and I are going to have to work out ourselves," she explained as she quickly changed out of her nightclothes and into the shirt and jeans.

"I just think—"

"I know what you think, but before we get lawyers involved I'd like—"

"I know." Farrah shook her head, grumbling, "You want to see if you two can come up with some type of agreement."

"That would be best for Alyia," Felicia added.

"Well, it's nice to see our sisterly connection is back on point." Farrah lowered her hands to her sides.

"Look, you have a meeting to get to and I have a call to make, so go. I'll be just fine." Felicia dismissed her with a wave. "Don't worry. I won't sign off on anything."

Farrah gave her a hard glare then sighed. "All right, I'll let you deal with the good doctor, but I won't be long." Farrah left her sister to finish getting dressed.

Felicia sat on the edge of her bed and dialed a number that was all too familiar to her.

"Good morning, Steven."

Steven Daniel was head of the CIA's Office of Medical Services, which was responsible for tracking potential medical threats to the United States. He and his team worked in collaboration with a number of different agencies, including the World Health Organization, and he was Felicia's boss.

"Good morning, Felicia. I need—"

"I know you need my answer, but I told you I need a little more time," she said more sharply than she'd intended.

"Stop trying to read my mind," he replied, his voice slightly rising. "I'm not one of your sisters."

"Sorry, sir. Stressful morning. What can I do for you?"

"I need you to reach out to Dr. Stacy Gray while you're in Atlanta."

Felicia sat straighter. "The new head of the CDC? Why, what's going on?"

"There's been an outbreak of Legionnaires' disease in New York, California, Illinois, Texas and now Georgia."

"That kind of disease can ravage the lungs quickly," she said. "Has it been contained?"

"We hope so," he replied, but his voice was haunted more so than she could ever recall it being before. "They've already issued warnings, so every hospital in the country is on alert. I've deployed teams in each state to start building an assessment of each case. While the CDC will take the lead in helping the states recover and restore public health functions, we have to find out how and why this happened."

"Let me guess. You want me to oversee the processing of the specimens when they come in," she said, falling back onto her bed. The idea of a massive outbreak happening right in her immediate vicinity was a scary proposition, more so now that she had Alyia.

"You *are* my expert and you're already in town," he reminded her.

"Yes, and I'm on maternity leave. I'm only in town to handle some family business," she countered.

"Well, this is the world's business, and you might as well get used to life-changing interruptions, because once you take over my job, it will be your new way of life," Steven explained, his voice flat.

Felicia wasn't sure she could handle any more life-changing interruptions now that she had a child. "I haven't accepted your job yet."

"We both know you will," he shot back. "You've dedicated your life to this work and worked your young ass off for this job—taking and solving assignments that have saved millions of lives. There is no one more qualified... and before you start with the seniority thing—"

"Look who's reading minds now."

Steven laughed. "All you've accomplished here in the last three years has been outstanding. We have folks here that haven't contributed one-fourth of what you have to keep the world safe. So of course you would be the logical and most appropriate person to take the job. How about this? As soon as you're done with this case, you can take a few more weeks off before your new assignment. You can get your apartment ready and get to know the team you'll be working with. I hear Paris is beautiful in January."

"Paris is beautiful any time of year," she agreed.

Steven sighed. "Well, there you go. You deserve this promotion."

"Thanks, but I have a lot to think about."

"Don't think too long," Steven said encouragingly. "My wife's past ready for me to retire."

Felicia laughed, repositioning on the bed. "When can I expect the first batch of cultures?"

"In a couple of days."

"Okay, thanks."

"Good luck," Steven said before ending the call.

Felicia dusted her face with a little powder and put on some lip gloss. She slipped her feet into a pair of black sandals, glanced in the mirror and said, "Here goes nothing."

She walked into the living room to find that Griffin had removed his suit coat and was now kneeling next to the playpen, talking to Alyia, and her heart skipped several beats. All the morning's dishes had been removed and Ms. Ellen was keeping a watchful eye on things from the kitchenette.

"Ms. Ellen, I think we'll have to take a trip to the children's museum on our next visit," Felicia announced.

"I understand. Would you like me to take Alyia so you and your friend can speak in private?"

Felicia could feel Griffin's eyes on her and her body was responding to his attention in a manner she wasn't used to. Embarrassment was burning a hole in her resolve. "No, I think we'll be fine. If we need you, we'll call out."

"Okay, then. She's full and dry, so she shouldn't be any trouble. I'll just go do a little reading." She left the kitchenette and came to stand next to the playpen. "It was nice meeting you, Griffin."

"Nice meeting you, too." Griffin watched as Ms. Ellen gave Alyia a kiss on the cheek, then disappeared down the hall.

Griffin, who was now sitting on the floor next to the playpen, patted the floor. "Care to join me?"

Felicia grinned and settled on the Berber carpet with her legs bent to the side.

They both sat in silence for several minutes and watched Alyia bounce herself up and down in her playpen. Her contentment made them both smile.

"So," Griffin finally said, locking a gaze on Felicia. "Looks like we have a daughter."

Chapter 12

Felicia wasn't sure if she should feel relieved or concerned by Griffin's seemly changed mood. "I guess it's safe to assume that you read the letter and reviewed the DNA test results?"

"You mean Valerie's so-called confession and apology letter?" Griffin asked, frowning. "Yes, I read it. I was more interested in the DNA results."

"I'm sure you were. You're welcome to take your own test, but I'm pretty sure she's your biological daughter," Felicia offered.

"I have no doubts. Look at her." Griffin turned his attention back to the baby who was now lying on her back, trying to put her foot in her mouth. "She looks like me… she even has my eyes."

Felicia laughed. "And your attention to detail, if I'm remembering correctly."

"What do you mean?" Griffin's eyes found hers and his eyebrows came to attention.

"You saw the way she played with her toys and her feet, examining every inch. It's like she has to know everything about them before she can put one in her mouth," she explained, smiling.

"Well, I don't blame her there. You can't go around just

putting anything in your mouth these days," he said, offering Felicia a sexy, suggestive smile.

Felicia's face, as well as other parts of her body, flamed at the thought of what she'd love to do to his mouth. "She's also easily bored," she said, breaking eye contact and changing the subject. "Which is what, now that she's sitting back up looking sleepy, tells me she'll be out soon—both traits of yours, too."

"Oh, really?"

"Yes, really. Remember Dr. Randall's class while we were waiting for our turn to present our project?" Felicia recalled a vivid image of him being so far into a nap that he'd nearly slid out of his chair.

Griffin threw his head back and laughed. "I can't believe you actually remember that. Anyway, I'd had a long night."

"I bet you did," she murmured.

"What was that?" Griffin asked.

"Never mind." Felicia reached into the playpen and laid Alyia down on her side. She pulled down a pink blanket and covered the sleeping baby.

"This has to be very strange for you, too," Griffin suggested.

"You have no idea."

"Then tell me about it," he whispered.

"Tell you what?" Felicia asked, taking a seat in a chair next to the playpen.

Griffin followed suit and positioned his over six-foot frame on the sofa across from her chair. "How did you find out about all of this...about *her*?" Griffin questioned, briefly looking at Alyia's sleeping form.

Felicia remained silent for a moment before saying, "That could take a minute."

Griffin sat back in his chair. "I've cleared my calendar and I'd really like to know everything, including more about the lovely Ms. Ellen, who's been taking care of my daughter."

His daughter. Two words that signaled a problem she was hoping not to have. Felicia went to the kitchenette and poured herself another cup of coffee. "Care to join me?" she offered, holding up the pot.

"Sure, black is fine. Thank you."

She returned and handed Griffin his cup, reclaiming her previous spot. She took several sips before she started explaining how their lives had suddenly intersected.

Twenty minutes into the conversation, Griffin said, "Wow...unbelievable. I don't know how I would have reacted at such news," he offered.

"Oh, I most certainly do," she countered. "You accused me of lying and being after your money, remember?"

"Oh, yeah, about that—"

"Don't worry about it." Felicia gave an unconcerned wave. "We all handle shock differently. I damn near passed out...you were rude," she teased with a grin.

Griffin looked away for a moment before meeting her gaze. "I sincerely apologize for my behavior."

"You're forgiven. Shall I continue?"

"Please..."

Felicia took another sip of her coffee before launching into the rest of the story.

Griffin exhaled. He was sitting forward with his elbows on his knees, resting his chin on his hands. "I'm not sure what to say...what to even think about all this." He dropped his hands and sat back. "So you knew she was my daughter the first time you saw her?"

"Yes."

"Then why did you wait so long to get in touch with me?" His voice rose slightly, a tinge of impatience in his tone.

"I tried to contact you *several* times and multiple ways.

You know this already." Felicia took both cups back to the kitchenette and placed them in the sink. "You didn't respond, which prompted my visit to last night's event."

Griffin came and stood in front of Felicia, his arms folded across his chest. "I never *got* any messages," he declared in a raised voice.

Felicia raised her chin, pushed her shoulders back and said, "*Not* my issue!"

They stood staring at each other for several moments. Alyia's deep-sleep sigh broke their silent standoff. They rushed to the playpen to find her still sleeping but lying on her back, smiling.

"Can I ask you a question?" Felicia whispered, keeping her eyes on Alyia and off the man who was sending waves of desire throughout her body.

"Of course," he replied, shifting his gaze to Felicia.

"Why did you do it? I know several of our friends did, and it was for a good cause and all, but you don't seem like the type to donate sperm," Felicia said, finding the strength to look him in those hypnotic gray eyes.

Griffin flinched. "I didn't donate my sperm. Not the way you think."

"What?"

He kept his voice low as he explained. "After Valerie's diagnosis and all that talk about young people and our mortality, it got me to thinking. What if something happened to *me*? There would be no part of me or our family left behind. I'm my parents' only child. So I decided to *store* my sperm, not *donate* it. But when I got to the clinic they started talking to me about using some of my deposit for stem cell research."

Felicia nodded, flicking a quick look toward Alyia. "That makes sense. Cell research was a big deal to you back then."

"Still is, and I love how you remember that." Griffin

smiled down at her. "The information on where the sperm could be found is in my will with my lawyer. The only people that knew what I'd done were the guys I'd gone with. I have no idea how Valerie found out about it or where it had gone."

"I think I can help with that. Valerie hooked up with your old roommate at the time. Didn't Todd make deposits on a regular basis because he needed the money?"

Griffin nodded and then his lips set in a thin line.

Felicia could almost see the light in his head flicker on. "Well, if he was one of the guys that went with you—"

"He was," Griffin confirmed.

"Then all he had to do was mention that to Valerie. The rest, as they say…"

"Unbelievable," he said, shaking his head.

"Can I ask you one more question?"

"Anything."

Felicia captured her lip between her teeth for a moment; she wasn't sure she really wanted to know the answer to the question. "What happened between you and Valerie? I mean, something had to have happened. Her obsession for you was too intense. She went through such extreme measures to have *your* child."

"I really don't know," he said, scratching his chin. "It wasn't that serious."

"What wasn't?"

"I'd finally worked up the nerve to ask you out after our brief career as dishwashers," he admitted, the corners of his mouth rising. "Remember that night?"

Felicia giggled. "I do."

"When I stopped by your place, Valerie beat me to the punch and asked me out. I told her I wasn't interested… as nicely as I could, of course, but I could see her feelings were hurt."

"Oh, no…"

Griffin shrugged. "She seemed fine, or at least she covered really well. She even said it was cool, that she just wanted someone that wasn't female to hang out with. But…"

"But what?" A crease appeared between her eyes.

"I think she figured out I was interested in you," he offered.

"How?"

"I brought you some calla lilies."

Felicia smiled. "You did?" she whispered.

"It was your favorite flower back then."

"Still is," she said.

"Valerie noticed the flowers and commented on how she knew they were your favorites."

"I don't remember getting anything from you."

Griffin nodded. "That's because I didn't leave them. I thought it might be awkward for you, especially if you weren't interested in me like I was in you."

"That's just it. I was—and Valerie knew it."

Griffin smiled. "You were?"

"Yes. I just wasn't interested in being part of a harem."

"A what?" he asked, frowning.

"Come on, now." Felicia gave him a sideways glance. "You were *dating* both Miriam and Santana from our lab group at the same time, and I use the term *dating* loosely."

Griffin's frown deepened. "What are you talking about? I didn't date anyone from our school, let alone our lab group. I never dated anyone I was taking a class with. Who told you…?" His eyes narrowed.

Felicia dropped her head in her hands and shook it.

"Valerie…" Griffin nearly growled.

Felicia nodded, keeping her head down. "She made me think you were a player," she explained through her hands. Shame and anger were circling Felicia like a fog; shame for not seeing through Valerie's manipulation and anger over their lost opportunity.

"So I guess you weren't dating someone from home, either."

"What?" Felicia dropped her hands and stared up into his eyes.

"Valerie told me you were with someone that worked for your father. That you only dated men that either worked with or for your family's company. Something about your dad checking out all the guys you date, so it'd just be easier if you dated someone he already knew. I'm not sure why I believed her, but I did."

All the guys... What guys? How could you? "No, I wasn't," she declared. "Is that why you didn't try to ask me out again?"

"Yes, and you have no idea how much I wanted to, too." They stared at each other in silence.

Griffin cupped Felicia's face with his right hand and ran his thumb slowly across her lips. Her breath caught and a shiver ran down her back. Griffin captured Felicia's chin between his thumb and index finger and began lowering his head when Alyia released a deep sigh. They both turned and looked at her.

Satisfied that Alyia was fine, and needing to put some space between her and Griffin, Felicia went to the refrigerator and pulled out a glass pitcher of sweet tea. "Would you like something to drink before I tell you the rest of the story? I can't have any more coffee."

"No, I'm fine," he replied, keeping his eye on Alyia, almost as if he needed to confirm everything he was feeling and experiencing was really happening.

Felicia wasn't sure if the moment she and Griffin had just shared would return, but she hoped that it would, that they'd get the chance to revisit an opportunity that they'd been denied. They both returned to their seats and Felicia continued to explain things as she knew them.

Chapter 13

"After everything she'd done, Valerie actually tried to have my daughter adopted?" Griffin nearly roared, gray eyes flashing with anger. He already knew the answer and wasn't expecting one.

"Yes, she figured we would be too busy to raise a child."

Griffin shifted his gaze to the little girl. He'd been dealing with a whirlwind of emotions as he'd sat and listened to Felicia recall her experiences about their child. The thought of some stranger raising her sent him to a place of fury he was fighting hard to contain.

Griffin stood and walked over to the playpen to stare down at his sleeping baby. Adoption? Foster care? She could've have landed in the care of people who had no clue of how much she would mean to him.

He rubbed his right knuckles in the palm of his left hand, trying to prevent an internal volcano from erupting. Then he felt a soft hand slowly slide down his back. With each stroke of that hand a sense of calm returned and in its place a yearning for the woman that hand belonged to emerged. After several moments his hands and shoulders lowered and his eyes closed, enjoying the sensation of her touch. It was a move few knew would work.

"We need you to stay calm," Felicia whispered, glancing down at Alyia.

"You remembered," he finally said, opening his eyes, then turning to face her before intertwining their hands.

"How could I forget? It was the only thing that stopped you from hurting that poor kid who'd accused you of stealing his idea for that project."

Griffin smiled and brought her right hand to his lips, placing a kiss on her inner palm and eliciting a slight tremble from her, a sign that she wanted him, too. "You were the one that finally got that little bastard to admit he lied. We made a great team back then." He pulled her closer to him, wrapping his arms around her waist.

"M-more like research and lab partners that became friends," Felicia stammered.

Griffin gifted her with a wide smile before looking over his shoulders at Alyia.

"Well, we're a team now, aren't we?"

"I guess so," Felicia acknowledged.

"Tell me the rest."

"You sure?" Felicia asked, shaking in his embrace.

"Might as well get it over with. Rip the Band-Aid off, so to speak."

Felicia laughed out loud but quickly pulled her right hand free and captured the sound with it.

"What?"

"That's what Farrah said we should have done about telling you the truth."

Griffin grinned. "Not sure how well that would've worked, either. What changed Valerie's mind about the adoption and finally telling the truth?"

Felicia pulled free and stepped away from Griffin to get her bearings. Running her hand up and down Griffin's muscled back to keep him calm, then him holding and kissing her hand, was wreaking havoc on her emotions, not to mention her body. Griffin was awakening both familiar and unfamiliar desires that she had to keep under control. They couldn't deal with an attraction right now. But she had to give him credit that he was a lot more accepting than he had initially been.

"The way John explained it, she simply ran out of time." Felicia and Griffin returned to their seats just as Griffin's phone beeped. He checked the message and returned it to his jacket pocket.

"Everything okay? You need to deal with that?"

"No," he replied. "If she was going to throw our child to the wind, how did we finally make the cut?" Griffin inquired, leaning back in his chair.

"It seems none of the couples she was considering were actually good enough. John reminded Valerie of her initial thoughts on me being the best caregiver. He was finally able to convince her that I was the best alternative."

"So we…" Griffin used his index finger to point between himself and Felicia. "In her mind, we're Alyia's best *alternative*, her biological father and one of the best women I know."

Felicia smiled and nodded at the compliment. "That's when John reached out to find me, which wasn't easy since I was working on the other side of the world."

"Ms. Ellen had been taking care of her all this time?" Griffin scratched his neatly trimmed beard. "I mean, before they reached out to you?"

"Yes, but you don't have to worry about Ms. Ellen. She's amazing with Alyia. She was just as surprised and appalled about what Valerie had done and was planning to do. Ms. Ellen raised three children of her own and she's enjoying helping out. That is, until she gets grandbabies of her own," Felicia said with a chuckle.

Griffin nodded slowly. "She really seems to love her."

"She does."

"Look—"

Griffin was interrupted by Alyia making her presence known with a loud whimper. Felicia and Griffin stood, but before they could act Ms. Ellen had made it through the door and was standing next to the playpen with a bottle in hand. "Nanny's here," she said, reaching into the playpen, picking up Alyia while Griffin and Felicia stood back and watched in awe at how quickly and easily the experienced woman handled the situation.

Felicia felt a shock of warmth in her hand but didn't look down to identify the source.

"Oh, I'm sorry." Ms. Ellen showed them Alyia's bottle. "Would you—?"

"No," they answered simultaneously.

Ms. Ellen's eyes swept over the couple and the corner of her mouth lifted. "Let's go get you changed," she said to Alyia who held her bottle as Ms. Ellen carried her from the room. Alyia popped it out just long enough to coo and gurgle at Felicia before putting it right back in.

"I still can't get used to the sound of her crying and that feeling of helplessness that comes with it," Felicia confessed.

"I can understand that," he said as Felicia noticed they were standing with their hands intertwined again.

Felicia looked up into Griffin's eyes and their gray tint had become slightly darker. He held her gaze then took the back of his free hand and ran it slowly down the side of her face. Felicia shivered and suddenly found it hard to inhale.

"Breathe, Felicia," he whispered.

She released a breath that she hadn't realized she had been holding. She pulled her hand free and took a step back.

"What is it that you need from me?" Griffin's voice had taken on a husky edge and he placed his hands in his pockets.

Felicia blinked twice before saying, "Excuse me?"

He gave her a slight grin. "At the party…you said you didn't want anything from me but you *needed* something. What was that?"

Felicia felt a sense of shame come over her. She had made the same assumption about Griffin that Valerie had made about them both. "Oh, that…"

Felicia took a moment to compose herself, but before she could give him her answer the door to the suite swung open.

"*You* still here?" Farrah said in a dry tone as she entered the suite.

Both Felicia and Griffin turned toward Farrah.

Griffin released an audible sigh of frustration and Farrah smiled.

Griffin returned his attention to Felicia and asked, "Have dinner with me tonight? We can finish talking then."

She hesitated only a split second before saying, "Yes, of course."

Griffin gifted Felicia with a wide smile. "How's eight?"

"Eight's fine."

"See you then," he said before slowly sliding his lips across her cheek, stopping at her lips where he gave her two soft but quick kisses. "One of those is for Alyia. See you in a few hours."

Felicia smiled and nodded.

Griffin headed for the door, stopping long enough to acknowledge her sister. "Farrah."

"Griffin," she replied as she held the door for him to exit.

"Well, damn. What did I miss?" Farrah asked, taking her sister's hand and dragging her to the sofa. "Sit… Spill."

"What? There's nothing to tell…not really."

"That kiss didn't look like nothing." Farrah smirked. "It actually looked kind of sweet."

The back of Felicia's hand found its way to her cheek on its own. "Yes, it was."

"Did you get his medical history? We don't want my wonderful niece to have to deal with some unexpected illnesses. Did you discuss any form of custody? Not that he has any legal rights to Alyia. Is he engaged?"

Farrah was hitting Felicia with rapid-fire questions and it was making her head spin. "No. We hadn't gotten to any of that yet."

"Well, what *did* you get to?" Farrah asked, her eyes narrowing.

"I just brought him up to speed on everything...how all this came about. I'm sure custody will be a topic of discussion this evening." *Especially if he didn't donate his sperm and has more rights than we initially thought.* That was a bit of information Felicia wasn't willing to share with Farrah in the moment.

"And the engagement?"

Felicia shrugged. "Who knows? That's not really my concern," she said with as much conviction as she could muster. For reasons she didn't want to explore, the very thought that he would soon be unavailable made her chest hurt.

"Sure, it's not," she taunted. "Do you need—?"

"I'm a big girl and we're both adults. I'm sure we'll be able to figure out what's best for our daughter."

"Our *daughter*..." Farrah echoed with one eyebrow raised. "Oh, now she's *our* daughter."

"Yes, she's our daughter, and I'm going to do what's best for her and I need your support."

Farrah glared at her sister in silence for several moments before pushing out a deep breath. "Fine, whatever you need, you know I'll do."

"Even if that means cutting Griffin a little slack?"

"If I must," she said, rising from the sofa. "But if he crosses the line even once—"

"I know. You will hurt him in ways he didn't even know was possible."

Farrah laughed. "This sibling mind-reading thing really does come in handy at times. Seriously, how much are you prepared to give?"

"I really don't know. I'm just taking things one step at a time."

"So I assume you're not leaving just yet." Farrah started removing the pins holding up her hair, dropping them on the table as she went.

"No. I have to work things out with Griffin before I go back home."

"Well, I can't stay, but I can come back in a day or two if you need me," she said, running her hands through her hair.

"Don't be ridiculous. I'm sure we'll have things wrapped up here in a few days and I'll be home before you know it. If I run into any problems, I'll call you, and you can bring in that heavy-hitter family lawyer you know."

Farrah sighed. "All right, but if you need me, I'm only a plane ride away."

"Seriously, you do know how old I am, right? Oh, wait…of course you do because we're the same age," she said, her sarcasm clear.

"Fine, I'll back off. Now, for the really important stuff." Farrah took her sister's hand and pulled her up off the sofa and down the hall toward the nursery. "First, we get my beautiful niece and her favorite sidekick ready, and then we're going shopping."

"Shopping?"

"Yes, I'm thinking a little Dior, Chanel and Vera Wang.

Definitely Vera, her daily-wear line is amazing. You're in desperate need of a serious wardrobe adjustment."

Felicia stopped short of the bedroom door. "My wardrobe is just fine, thank you very much."

"Yeah, for the lab or some remote hospital in Timbuktu."

Felicia threw her head back and laughed. "I guess jeans and a nice blouse won't cut it tonight?"

Farrah shuddered.

"I guess we're going shopping." Felicia reluctantly agreed.

Chapter 14

Griffin entered his three-story mansion and took the marble stairs two at a time, heading to the second-floor living area, when he heard a familiar sound coming from his kitchen. He dropped his head and gave it is a slow shake before heading back downstairs. He passed his formal living room and entered his massive gourmet kitchen. The black-and-white Italian marble and stainless-steel industrial appliances would make any chef smile. Griffin walked in to find his mother and Jia sitting at the eight-person island sharing a bottle of wine.

"There you are, son. Where *have* you been?" his mother asked, offering her cheek for his usual greeting.

"You know that spare key I gave you is for emergencies, right?" Griffin kissed both his mother and Jia on the cheek before saying, "I went to visit an old friend."

His mother's eyes narrowed and she waved off his complaint. "Anyone I know?"

"As a matter fact, yes. Do you remember my old classmate from medical school, Felicia Blake? Well, it's Dr. Felicia Blake now."

Lin Kaile offered Griffin a tight smile, cutting her eyes to Jia before returning them to her son. "Yes, of course. How is she?"

"Beautiful," he whispered as he reached for a glass to pour himself some wine from the bottle of Merlot they were sharing. "She's doing great…exceptionally, in fact."

"Was there any particular reason you went to see her?" Jia asked as she sipped her wine. Her insecurities were on full display.

"She and her sister came to the party last night and we didn't have a chance to catch up. I wanted to see her before she leaves."

"And did you?" Jia asked, reaching for the bottle of wine to top off her glass. "Catch up, I mean."

"When is she leaving?" his mother interjected.

Griffin looked at his mother before he turned his attention to Jia. "Somewhat, but we still have a few things to clear up." Griffin turned to his mother. "I'm not sure how long she'll be here."

"She's a doctor. I'm sure she has patients she needs to get back to," Jia intoned, pushing her glass to the side as if she suddenly didn't like the taste and folding her arms.

"Felicia's not that type of doctor. She's more of a research scientist that works for the CIA."

"That's all the more reason for her to get back home," his mother declared.

Griffin knew that his mother had always had an issue with his "going nowhere crush" on Felicia, as she called it. She believed that Felicia's ambition would always take precedence over family life. He wouldn't be surprised if she was blocking their connection. Griffin folded his arms and leered at his mother. "Felicia said she tried to reach out to me several times. In between Carol—the assistant you chose and insisted I hire—screening my calls and emails at the office and the fact I know you're always here trying to do the same, I'm lucky I get any non-hospital-related calls at all."

His mother shrugged. "The important people have your

private cell number," she said, raising her glass to her red lips.

Too bad I didn't have that number on my business cards; another one of your ideas, Mother, if I remember correctly.

"Griffin, your mother and Carol are only trying to stop the nonsense from getting through. You're a very wealthy man and some people—I'm not saying your friend is one of them, but some—will always try to take advantage of people in your position."

Griffin looked over at Jia. "The key word in that statement is *man,* and I'm more than capable of taking care of myself." He turned to his mother. "So, Mother, did you block Felicia's calls?"

His mother gave a nonchalant wave. "Probably, but I don't recall. What does it matter, anyway? It clearly wasn't professional. Otherwise, she would've gone through the hospital."

Griffin took a deep breath and exhaled slowly. "Mother, I need you to stop. And I'm going to remind Carol that she works for me, and if she wants to keep working for me, she'd better stop working for you."

"You're overreacting just like your father. Besides, what did that woman have to say that's so important you're actually chastising your mother?"

A smile slowly spread across his face. *Only that you have a grandchild.* "You'll know soon enough. In the meantime, can you please give me and Jia some privacy? We need to talk."

Griffin escorted his mother to her waiting Bentley that had arrived only minutes after she'd called for it. He walked back inside to find that Jia had brought their glasses and another bottle of wine into the living room. She'd removed her shoes, had let her hair down and was seductively lying across the extra-long, light-gray-and-white sofa. From the sexy smile and the way she batted her eyes, Griffin knew where Jia thought their evening was headed.

It seemed his lack of a proposal and their discussion about them not being on the same page when it came to their dating relationship hadn't been clear enough. Griffin knew he had to be more direct—rip the Band-Aid off. He needed to make sure his position with Jia was crystal clear and final before he could begin to approach Felicia with his plans for Alyia. He had to say the words. Tell her that their relationship was over and that his feelings were elsewhere.

Jia handed Griffin his wineglass. "You really have to take it easy on your mother. You know how protective she can be," she said, leaning back into the sofa.

Griffin sat on the love seat across from her. "Thanks," he said, accepting the glass. "I know. Look, Jia, we need to talk."

"Of course, but why are you sitting over there?" Jia patted the spot next to her. "Why don't you join me over here?"

Griffin set his wineglass on the small, round, glass coffee table between the two seats. "I'm fine here, thanks."

"Griffin, darling, what's wrong?"

"Jia, we discussed this last night, but I don't think you understood me."

Jia reached for her glass and took a sip. "Of course I did. You're not ready to get engaged right now. And I get that. You're taking on a big role at the hospital and now's not the time for another big, life-altering change."

Too late for that. "Yes, but I also said that I didn't think we had a future together."

"Yes, right now," she said, frowning as if Griffin couldn't understand the words coming out of her mouth.

"No, Jia, not ever. I care for you, and you know that.

We have a great time together, but we both agreed to keep things light."

Jia swept her feet off the sofa and sat straighter. "Yes, but that was before."

"Before what, exactly?"

"All the talk about marriage...developing a strong partnership," she said, her brows coming together.

Griffin went and sat next to her on the sofa. He took her hand in his and stared into her eyes. "Have you and I ever had any such conversation?"

"N-no...but..." she stammered, her frown deepening.

"But what?" he asked, matching Jia's confused look.

"Your mother and I have."

"You and my mother," he said, releasing her hand, unable to hide the disdain in his voice.

"Yes. She said it was time, you were ready, and that I needed to be sure I was ready, too," she explained.

"But you and I have never even talked about taking our relationship any further than where we are now. Why would you talk to my mother, rather than to me, if that's what you wanted?" he queried.

"I...I don't know. She mentioned it and I thought maybe she was right. Maybe the time had come."

"For what, exactly?"

"Marriage, kids, the whole thing." Jia leaned in and tried to kiss Griffin, but he stopped her attempt with his hand as the image of Felicia holding his child popped into his head.

"Jia, I'm sorry, but this—" he waved his hand between them "—isn't going to happen."

Jia leaned back. "What?"

"You know I care about you—"

"And I care for you, too," she said, reaching for his hand.

Griffin gave her hand a quick squeeze before he stood

and started pacing the room. He didn't want to hurt her, but he knew the next sentence out of his mouth would not only hurt Jia but bring the wrath of his mother down upon him. Griffin had always loved and respected his parents, and while he gave his mother a hard time, he knew she was only acting out of love for her only child. He could only hope that one day she'd see that he was only doing the same. Griffin stopped and faced an anxious-looking Jia.

"I'm sorry, but I can't marry you. Not now...not ever."

Jia sat in silence for several moments before asking, "Is it that doctor? The one you went to medical school with... had a crush on?" She folded her arms.

Griffin sighed. "Honestly, Jia, it's a lot of things, but Felicia showing up the way she did didn't help."

Griffin wasn't prepared to share the news about Alyia yet. He was still getting used to the idea that he was a father and wanted to figure out what impact this revelation could have on his life and any potential relationship with Felicia. If Cooper was right, things could get really complicated.

Jia reached for her shoes. As she slipped her feet into them she said, "You once told me that you had a crush on her, but you two were going in different directions. Remember that?" she asked, standing and reaching for her purse.

"I remember."

"Well, the way I see it, not much has changed in that regard. She works overseas, travels around the world." Jia used her right hand to pat Griffin on his heart before she let it rest there. "I'd hate for you to throw away something that could've been great for a what-if."

Griffin removed her hand from his heart and said, "I'm a doctor. I live in a world of what-ifs."

Jia took a step toward the door then looked over her

shoulder. "Call me when she leaves. Maybe I'll answer. And mark my words…she will leave."

"Not if I can help it," he murmured as he watched her sashay out the door.

Griffin retrieved his phone and dialed Cooper. "Well…"

Cooper explained Griffin's legal position and options regarding his rights to Alyia. When their call ended, Griffin decided to keep what he knew to himself. He was hoping to resolve things between him and Felicia without having to officially involve their lawyers or having to explain just how weak her position as Alyia's mother really was.

Felicia stood in a conference room behind a glass wall, looking out into one of the largest and most respected labs in the country as she waited for her meeting to begin with the newly appointed head of the CDC.

According to Steven, I'm going to be dealing with a life of interruptions. Add in the dangerous aspect of the job and I wonder, is that something I really want to deal with, now that I have Alyia? But I've worked so hard for this opportunity. I'm sure I'll be able to figure it out.

"Sorry to keep you waiting, Dr. Blake, but my last meeting ran long," Dr. Stacy Gray announced as she entered the room. The tall, slim brunette with short, curly hair and smooth, dark brown skin, wearing white scrubs and black pearls, offered her hand in greeting.

Felicia accepted it, briefly distracted by Stacy's black nail polish. "Please, call me Felicia, and it's a pleasure to meet you, Dr. Gray."

"It's Stacy, and the feeling is mutual. I've heard nothing but great things about you. Our president speaks very highly of you."

"He's very kind." Felicia could feel her face warming. "Congratulations on your appointment."

"Thank you. Let's sit," she said, gesturing toward the

conference table and chairs. "Sorry to interrupt your personal time off. I understand you have a new baby. Congratulations!"

"Thank you. I'm still getting used to things," she said.

"Are you sure you're ready to get back to work?"

While Felicia had enjoyed spending the last few weeks getting to know her daughter, the call of the lab was strong. "My work is important to me…to the country, and I can't turn my back on it."

"Good. Steven tells me you'll be supervising our work with the Legionnaires' situation."

"Oh, no," Felicia insisted. "I'm here to offer my assistance, that's all. You have an excellent team here. I've worked with many of them."

Stacy slanted her head slightly. "I've heard that…and on cases that we were struggling with, too."

Felicia shrugged. "In my current role, I'm privy to things that can help save time in resolving many mysteries."

"Oh, I think there's a bit more to it than that. You have quite the reputation in the field of biochemistry," she retorted.

Where is she going with this? "As do you."

Stacy smiled, reached into her pocket and pulled out a set of key cards and a temporary ID badge. She slid them across the table to Felicia. "Those keys give you access to everything you need on this floor, as well as get you into the building. Please wear your CIA photo ID. Steven says you have one."

"Yes, of course." Felicia picked up the key cards and ID.

Stacy stood. "We should have the first set of samples for you tomorrow."

"No problem. I'm looking forward to working with you."

Stacy offered up a lopsided grin. "As am I. I'm curious to see you in action," she replied before taking her leave.

Felicia looked down at the key cards again. "This should be interesting."

Later that afternoon, Felicia prepared for her evening with Griffin. She stared at the image before her, wearing a simple, deep green sheath dress with a scoop neck where her breasts stood proudly at attention. The dress hugged her body like a lover taking claim to what was his. Felicia looked past her mirror reflection and over her shoulder. "You think this is too much?"

"Oh, no," Ms. Ellen said, entering the room and holding a laughing Alyia on her hip. "You look beautiful, and this little one agrees."

Felicia turned away from the mirror to face her visitors. Alyia stretched out her arms and twisted her body away from her caregiver, clearly wanting her mother's attention. Felicia's heart exploded with joy as she reached for her daughter.

Alyia laughed as Felicia held her and patted her back. "Thank you. It's just I haven't worn anything so...obvious before."

"Obvious?" Ms. Ellen sat in a chair across from Felicia's bed.

"Like I'm trying to impress him or something."

"Impress him?" she said, frowning. "He's the one that needs to impress you."

"You're so sweet, Ms. Ellen," she said, kissing Alyia's neck. Felicia loved how that made her laugh and fling her hands about. They had come a long way from that first moment when they'd seen each other.

"Why would you have to impress Dr. Griffin? I mean, you're a wealthy and successful doctor in your own right."

"I don't. Not really. He just...he makes me feel like I do."

"Oh," she sang. "Let me have that little one. We don't want her to mess up your pretty new dress." Felicia kissed Alyia on the cheek and handed her over. "So you like him. That's good. It will make raising this beautiful one together much easier."

"I don't like him," she said, quickly lowering her head.

Ms. Ellen laughed. "Child, who you trying to convince? I may not be married anymore, but I know heat when I see it."

"We're just friends and now parents." Felicia checked her watch and started to gather her things.

"It doesn't have to stay that way, you know. I saw the way he looked at you. There's definitely something there." She offered a knowing smile.

Felicia gave a nonchalant shrug, not wanting to go there. Just the idea of Griffin wanting anything more with her was a complication she wasn't sure she was ready for. "I shouldn't be late."

"No worries. After I put this little one down, I think I'll do a little more reading before I turn in," she said as the doorbell rang.

"Right on time." Felicia kissed Alyia on the top of her head and Ms. Ellen on her cheek as the two continued to rock. "Good night, you two."

Felicia left the room after giving herself a final once-over and went to let Griffin in, a move she knew was about to change her life; only she didn't know just how much. For a detail-oriented scientist, that lack of information was unnerving.

Chapter 15

Griffin stood staring down at Felicia with his heart in his stomach and his manhood trying to get his attention. His eyes swept her body from head to toe. Her subtle makeup only enhanced her natural beauty. The dress she wore showed off her perfectly fit body and the color brought out the green in her hazel eyes. Her long, curly hair hung down her back perfectly. Felicia's bright smile, with a hint of amusement, finally registered.

"I'm sorry, did you say something?" Griffin asked, placing his hands in the pockets of his black Armani suit. He didn't trust himself not to act on his desire to kiss her in that moment.

Felicia laughed, and the sound had Griffin's body humming. "Yes, I said good evening."

"Good evening to you, too. You look breathtakingly beautiful."

Felicia's smile widened. "Thank you. You look quite handsome yourself."

"This old thing," he offered in jest. "Is Alyia asleep yet?"

"Ms. Ellen's putting her down now. Would you like to see her?"

"Yes, but when we return." Griffin offered Felicia his arm. "Shall we?"

The short limo ride to one of Atlanta's most popular steakhouses was a true test of endurance for Griffin. From the moment they sat down mere inches from each other, he had to remind himself that Felicia was not his. That he had no right to pull her onto his lap. To kiss her at the base of her neck and shoulders before finding her lips. To suck and tease her mouth before kissing her until they were both out of breath. He certainly didn't have any right to order his driver to raise the partition and drive around downtown Atlanta for at least an hour so he could explore the delicacies Felicia had always hidden under unflattering scrubs. No, Griffin knew those weren't his rights, so he sat still and choked out small talk until they reached their destination.

Griffin held his right hand at the small of Felicia's back as they entered the restaurant that sat on top of one of Atlanta's tallest downtown buildings. He only hoped that the arrangements he'd made wouldn't make Felicia uncomfortable, but he knew their discussion required privacy. Griffin also knew being alone with Felicia at his place was a level of intimacy both weren't quite ready for yet.

The empty rooftop restaurant, its floor-to-ceiling windows offering three-hundred-sixty-degree views of downtown, was spectacular. The single wood table with its large, leather-backed chairs was surrounded by expensive works of art.

"Are you sure they're open?" Felicia asked, her eyes scanning the room.

"Positive."

A long-legged brunette, wearing a tight black minidress and a big smile on her face, approached them. "Good evening, Dr. Kaile. Nice to see you again." She leaned in, kissing him on the cheek.

"Good evening, Kathy. I didn't realize you were working tonight."

"Yeah, well, as soon as I realized it was you that bought out the place for the night, including buying dinner at our sister restaurant for those people that might have been inconvenienced…well, I just had to see the reason why," she informed, her eyes giving Felicia a slow once-over before returning to Griffin. "I just knew you were finally proposing to what's-her-name. I guess by the looks of things you've moved on…yet again."

"Good evening. I'm Felicia Blake."

Griffin smiled at Felicia. *Always the peacemaker.* "Forgive my manners. Dr. Felicia Blake…Kathy Manor. Kathy and I are old friends," he explained.

"Yes, very old friends," Kathy offered, the bitterness in her voice dropping the temperature in the room several degrees. "Everything is as you requested. Shall I show you to your table?"

Both Felicia and Griffin's eyes traveled to the single-table setup. "That won't be necessary," Griffin answered. "I think we can find our way."

"Fine, Morris will be out shortly," she replied before making her exit, allowing the warmth back into the room.

"Wow, that was…awkward."

Griffin sighed. "Kathy and I went out on a few dates," he said, taking her hand as he led her to their table.

"You don't say. I assume things didn't end well."

"It was a long time ago." Griffin lifted a bottle of Chardonnay from the bed of ice in which it had been resting. "Care for a glass?"

"Yes, please."

Griffin used the corkscrew that had been left for his use and then poured an equal amount into two wineglasses. He handed one to Felicia and raised his. "To our future."

"Whatever that might be," Felicia added before taking a sip.

A slow smile spread across Griffin's face. He knew exactly what their future held. Now Griffin only had to convince Felicia to go along with his plans.

As Felicia stood looking out over the city, she was suddenly very grateful to Farrah for insisting on taking her shopping. She would've hated meeting Kathy, one of what had to be many of Griffin's ex-lovers, in one of her own unflattering outfits.

Griffin came and stood next to Felicia. "Your wine okay? I know how much you enjoyed some Chardonnay every now and then."

"It's delightful, thank you." Felicia looked down into her glass.

"You sure? Because you've hardly touched it."

"Well, I've never been much of a drinker," she said.

"I know." Griffin offered a small smile. "We'll have a few courses, but I hope you don't mind that for our main meal I've asked the chef to prepare this steak and pasta dish that he's famous for. It's quite delicious."

"I'm a vegetarian now," she said, her face expressionless.

"Oh, I'm sorry. I'm sure—"

Felicia started laughing.

"What?"

"Griffin, I'm teasing you. Sorry, bad joke, I guess. I'm just a little nervous. That actually sounds great."

Griffin smiled. "No problem. I'm a little nervous, too. It's not every day you sit down to discuss custody arrangements with the mother of your child. A child neither of you ever knew existed."

"I guess not," Felicia turned away from the window and walked around the room, examining the expensive works of art on display. She wasn't sure how she felt about Griffin closing the restaurant just so they could talk. "It really wasn't necessary to buy out the restaurant tonight. I'm sure we would have had enough privacy."

"Not really. I'm pretty popular these days, especially after the announcement was made regarding my new job. It seems everywhere I go now people either want to congratulate me or schedule an appointment. Tonight I don't want any interruptions."

Felicia nodded. "I understand. Shall we sit…talk?"

"Of course," Griffin said, pulling out Felicia's chair for her.

"Such a gentleman," she said, taking her seat.

Griffin leaned forward, his lips grazing Felicia's ear as he said, "I do try." The warmth of Griffin's breath had Felicia gripping the stem of her wineglass a little tighter, and she had the sudden desire to cross her legs.

Griffin moved around the table and took a seat. "More wine?"

"No, I'm fine." *No, you are not. Get it together, girl.* "So what do you have in mind?"

A slow, sexy smile eased across his face. "About what exactly?" he asked, leaning in closer as though they were actually in a crowded restaurant and Felicia couldn't hear him.

Griffin's scent assaulted Felicia's senses, forcing her to give in to her desire to slowly cross her legs; she needed the small relief that move offered. Felicia might not have had sex before, but she knew what it was to desire a man, this man in particular, and her body certainly knew what it needed.

Felicia cleared her throat and said, "Alyia's custody."

Chapter 16

Griffin was hoping to hold off a little longer before having this conversation. Before he could respond, the chef appeared, a male waiter following behind him holding a tray with two large plates of food. "Welcome back, Doctor G, and good evening, beautiful lady. I'm Chef Morris Gill," the tall, dark-skinned gentleman with a medium build introduced himself.

"Good evening," Felicia replied.

"Thanks for doing this." Griffin stood and offered his hand. "We really appreciate it."

"Any time," he said, accepting Griffin's handshake. "It's not often I accept these types of requests, but for you and your family…anything."

Griffin nodded and turned his attention back to Felicia. "Chef Morris also owns four other restaurants around Atlanta."

"That's wonderful. I'll have to check them out the next time I'm in town."

Griffin shot Felicia a look that had her eyes widening slightly in response. Their exchange must've made Chef Morris uncomfortable because he quickly waved the waiter forward and a plate with multiple types of hors d'oeuvres was placed before them. "For your first course, we have a few of my favorite things for you to sample—Oysters Rockefeller, grilled bacon wrapped around jalapeño-and-cheese-stuffed shrimp and seared steak in lettuce cups."

"They look and smell delicious," Felicia said, using her hand to wave the scents forward. "They're all my favorite things, too."

"Enjoy," Chef Morris said before leaving.

Felicia took a sip of her wine. "About the custody—"

Griffin took his seat. "How about we save that conversation for a little later? Instead I'd like to hear more about you." He reached for a small plate and handed it to Felicia.

Felicia accepted the plate and started selecting her appetizers. "All right, what do you want to know?"

"How about something easy? Tell me about your family's business. I took your sister's advice and I looked you up—your company, anyway." Griffin smiled. "I knew you came from a successful family, Felicia, but I had no idea just how successful."

"Obviously you know my family owns an international security systems and private investigation firm, Blake and Montgomery." Felicia took a bite of her shrimp.

"Where did the Montgomery come from?" Griffin placed two of each item on his own plate.

"My father started the business with his best friend and Army Ranger buddy, Milton Montgomery, my brother-in-law Meeks's father, and they just decided to name the business after themselves." She smiled.

Griffin nodded as he finished chewing his food. "Your dad was an Army Ranger? Now, that's impressive."

"According to our mother, Dad was something else back in the day, in a good way. I used to love hearing his war stories being told by his army buddies."

"He let you hear them?" he asked, frowning.

"Of course not. We eavesdropped. Farrah's idea, of course."

Griffin laughed. "Why doesn't that surprise me? What happened to Meeks's father? There wasn't much about him online."

"It was a long time ago but his dad was hit by a car crossing the street. Such a senseless accident," she explained, lowering her head. Felicia sighed.

"I'm sorry to hear that. It must be hard losing a parent in such a way," Griffin said.

"It was. In fact, it was hard on everyone, especially my dad. The Blake and Montgomery clans had always been close…like family."

"Hence his and your sister Francine's marriage," he suggested.

Felicia nodded. "But that was years in the making."

"Really? Tell me about it." Griffin took another bite of his food.

"You really want to know this?"

"We're getting to know each other, remember." Griffin reached for his wine and took a drink.

"Excuse the intrusion, but if you're ready, we can remove these dishes. I have your soup and salad," the waiter said, another, smaller gentleman at his side.

Griffin gestured with his hand for Felicia to provide the response. "Sure, thank you."

The other man cleared their used dishes so bowls of potato soup and Spanish salad could be placed in front of them. Once their water and wineglasses had been topped off, both men retreated.

"I don't know if I'll have room for the main course after this," Felicia admitted.

"You'll still have to leave room for dessert."

"There's always room for dessert," she said before tasting her soup. "Um…this is fantastic."

"Yes, it is," he said, lowering his spoon. "So, Meeks and Francine…"

"I think they had been in love with each other for years. I know for a fact that Meeks has always had a thing for my sister. As a matter of fact, besides our parents, he was the only one who could tell us apart." Felicia took another spoonful of her soup.

"I can tell *you* apart from Farrah," he proudly proclaimed.

"Yes, you can," she replied.

Griffin figured Felicia would be close to her sisters, but to hear her speak so lovingly about her whole family and even her extended relatives just confirmed what he'd always known and debunked his mother's assumptions; in fact, family would always come first with Felicia.

"As kids, it was much harder, since we all had the same eye color."

"Green, right?"

"Yes."

"At what age did it change? Your eyes, I mean." Griffin wondered at the idea.

"It started when we turned thirteen, when we hit puberty. Francine's eyes stayed green, Farrah's blue and mine—" she blinked several times "—are—"

"Beautiful...hazel with green specks."

Felicia smiled. "Anyway, Meeks never acted on his feelings for Francine. They danced around their feeling and drove each other, and the rest of us, crazy with their disagreements about everything, especially the business. Instead of dealing with his feelings, Meeks just became this overprotective guardian that he thought Francine needed. It got worse when she joined the company. Then she got hurt—"

"Hurt?"

"She was shot while working. While it wasn't life-threatening, to Meeks it was. It sent him into a tailspin."

"Apparently they worked it out. They're married and

she's expecting…twins, right? I read an article online speculating about it," he said.

"It wasn't easy, and they had a few hurdles to get over, but, yes, they did and they are." A proud smile spread across Felicia's face.

This woman is amazing, beautiful inside and out. I couldn't ask for a better mother for my daughter…or woman for myself.

"Ready for the main course?" Chef Morris asked as he approached their table. He presented them each with a large, square plate with a medium-rare, butterfly piece of steak topped with a shrimp and crabmeat dressing, on a bed of pasta.

"Wow, that looks beautiful and smells wonderful." Felicia complimented him.

"Thank you. Ring this—" Morris pulled a small brass bell from his pocket and placed it on the table "—when you're ready for dessert. No one will disturb you until we hear the bell. I guess I'll leave you two to it." The chef and his waiter disappeared in the direction from which they'd come.

"Bon appétit," Griffin said before digging into his meal.

Felicia took a bite of her food. The steak, with a bit of dressing and pasta, just seemed to melt in her mouth. She closed her eyes and moaned as she enjoyed the perfectly cooked meat bursting with flavor. The one thing Felicia had always enjoyed about her many travels was the delicious delicacies she got to experience. She was a self-proclaimed foodie.

Felicia slowly opened her eyes to find Griffin staring at her, specifically her mouth. "Sorry. I've got a thing for good food," she explained as she took another bite.

"I think I have a thing for watching you enjoy it." His voice had taken on a husky tone.

Their eyes collided. Griffin put down his fork, pushed back his chair and stood. Felicia's gaze followed his every movement. He came to stand next to her. "Put your fork down," he ordered. Felicia complied, trembling slightly with anticipation.

Griffin pulled back her chair, took Felicia's hand and drew her in his arms. The sudden movement made her grip his broad shoulders as she raised her head slightly to maintain eye contact.

"You are simply breathtaking and I can't wait a second longer to do this."

Griffin leaned forward slowly, keeping his eyes on Felicia's as he ran his tongue across her lips before capturing them in a passionate kiss.

The kiss whipped Felicia's body into a raging, out-of-control inferno, an overwhelmingly unique experience for her. Her arms made their way around his neck and she pressed against him. Felicia's body was demanding something she had been denying herself for years, and while she knew they had a lot to discuss, the only talking she wanted to do was with their bodies. And, evidently, he felt the same way.

Felicia could feel Griffin's desire as her hips swayed against him. Griffin's hold had tightened and his right hand gripped her butt; it was a sensual dance that continued as he kissed and sucked her lips and neck. Felicia was so lost in this new experience that she'd forgotten they were in public, and so had the fiercely private Griffin. The sound of breaking glass managed to penetrate the haze of desire they'd been trapped in. They both turned toward the sound.

"Kathy," Griffin acknowledged, stepping in front of Felicia. "I thought you left."

Kathy's eyes zeroed in on Griffin's pants before returning to his face. "And I thought you had more class," she grumbled, bending to pick up the tray and the shards of glass.

"Let me help you," Griffin offered.

"No, I got it. I'm sure you want to get back to your groping—I mean food." Kathy picked up all the broken pieces of glass and the tray and quickly left.

Felicia knew she should be embarrassed by her wanton behavior, but she wasn't. However, she thought she should apologize, because she had no idea what had come over her.

"Sorry about—"

"I'm sorry—"

They both smiled. It appeared apologizing was just one more thing they wanted to do together.

Chapter 17

Griffin was hard as granite while he sat and tried to enjoy the rest of their meal. His desire for Felicia was stronger than he'd allowed himself to remember. They chose not to discuss their less-than-stellar behavior or Kathy's response to it. Instead they tried their hand at small talk, mostly about their work.

Chef Morris emerged from the kitchen with a single, square plate with several desserts from which to choose. Griffin passed while Felicia selected the red-velvet cheesecake. Griffin watched in awe as she consumed her dessert with the same sense of satisfaction as with her meal. Felicia licking frosting from her fork was a move that only escalated Griffin's desire for her.

"Are we really going to sit here and pretend what happened didn't happen?" Griffin asked.

Felicia placed her fork across the top of her plate. "I guess not."

"I want to apologize. I let my suppressed attraction for you—"

"Your what?" she inquired, slanting her head slightly.

Felicia's confused expression made Griffin smile. "Come on, you had to know that I had the biggest crush on you in school."

"And exactly *how* would I know that?" A line appeared between her brows. "You treated me like a colleague…just another student, or worse, a sister. You never showed any romantic interest toward me."

"I guess my courtship was a little subtle," he conceded, scratching his chin.

"Subtle," she scoffed. "How about nonexistent?"

"So the back and foot rubs I gave you quite often or playing with your hair weren't clues? I had to find ways to touch you," he confessed.

"You gave all the women in our group back and foot rubs, usually to keep us awake and going so we could finish our projects," Felicia countered.

"Well, I know I didn't play with anyone else's hair. And I didn't run the back of my hand down anyone's face as they began to fall asleep on a table in the library," Griffin reminded Felicia, reaching across the table, taking her hand in his and intertwining their fingers. The warmth that spread through his body was a sweet reminder of the feelings this woman could easily invoke in him. Their eyes met. "You do remember that, don't you? Or was I in *that* moment alone, too?"

"I think we need to talk about Alyia," she whispered, sighing as she pulled her hand free. "That is why we're here."

Griffin sat back in his chair and pushed out a quick breath. "Sure. When you and your sister found me at the event, you said you needed something from me. What was that exactly?" he asked, sliding the napkin from his lap onto his empty plate.

"Your medical history and something I wouldn't consider asking you for now," Felicia said, holding his gaze.

"Let me guess." Griffin folded his large arms across his chest. "You didn't want me to challenge you for custody of Alyia. You simply wanted me to walk away. You know that's not going to happen, right?"

"I wouldn't ask at this point."

"Why would you ask at *any* point?" he challenged. "Do I seem like the kind of man that would walk away from his own flesh and blood? Would you?"

Felicia raised her chin and matched his move. "Of course not. I'm her mother now."

Griffin leaned forward slightly. "And I'm her father."

Felicia's shoulders dropped and she released a deep sigh. "Look, Griffin, I apologize for making assumptions about you. The same assumption Valerie made about us."

Griffin nodded.

"I just didn't know what to expect, or do, for that matter."

A slow smile spread across Griffin's face. "Good thing I do."

Felicia reached for her water and took several sips, trying to calm herself; Griffin's mischievous smile was sending lightning bolts to areas of her body that had been dormant for a while. "What might that be?" she asked, sitting back in her chair.

"We get married."

Felicia roared with laughter to the point that tears formed then streaked down her face. When Griffin didn't follow suit, the laughter trickled to a halt. Her eyes scanned his face, looking for signs that he'd been joking. When she saw none, she gave her head a small shake. Felicia thought she had to have misheard him. "Excuse me?"

Griffin leaned forward and took Felicia's left hand in his. "You heard me. I think we should get married."

"That's what I thought you said," a wide-eyed Felicia replied. "Why?"

"To give Alyia the family she deserves."

Felicia pulled her hand free, pushed back her chair and stood. "We don't have to get married for that," she said before making her way over to the window. She stared out at the city skyline, covered with stars, trying to bring herself under control. She needed space; she couldn't think with Griffin holding her hand and looking at her as though she was another helping of that delicious meal they'd consumed earlier.

Griffin came up behind Felicia. He wasn't touching her but he was close enough that she could feel the heat radiating from his body. Felicia resisted the urge to lean back into him. "Felicia, people get married for all kinds of reasons. I can't see any better reason than wanting to raise our daughter...*together*, in a proper home."

Felicia turned and looked up at him. "Griffin we *can* raise our daughter, together, without getting married. We barely know each other."

"That's not true—"

"No, we knew the people we used to be...the students," she said, walking around him and exploring the room.

Griffin watched her make tracks. "I followed your career for years, as I suspect you followed mine."

"That's professional curiosity," she said, stopping her stride. Felicia tapped her fingers on their table. "That has nothing to do with making a lifelong commitment."

"Bull." Griffin walked slowly toward her, saying, "There's always been something between us. We just weren't in the position to do anything about it."

"Physical attraction isn't reason enough to get married, either."

Griffin smirked. "For some, it's the only reason."

"Well, we're not those kinds of people." Felicia picked up her water glass and took several sips. "Be serious about this—"

"I am. We have a lot in common *and* we're attracted to each other. I think that's a great place to start."

"What about…love?" she asked, biting her bottom lip and looking up into his eyes. "Don't you want a real marriage?"

Griffin ran the index finger of his right hand slowly across Felicia's lips, releasing them from their ivory prison, and she trembled. "Oh, this will be a real marriage. That I can promise you."

"There's more to marriage than having a consistent source for sex," she shot back. "It's much more than that. It's what my sisters have…my parents, and I'm not going to sell myself short for anything less."

"I understand how you feel—"

"Do you?" Her brows snapped together. "My African-American and Hispanic father grew up in Spanish Harlem, while my Irish-American mother grew up in Manhattan. Talk about being from different worlds, yet my mother said she took one look at my father and knew she'd love him for the rest of her life."

"Wow, how did they meet?"

"Mom was out with friends at a club in Harlem. She said he stood out." Felicia laughed. "She may have known that Dad was The One, but what she didn't count on was him giving her three babies at once—girls at that, too."

"Do you think your dad was ever disappointed about not having sons?"

Felicia shook her head. "Not at all. Dad taught us everything he would a boy."

Griffin tilted his head slightly. "Such as?"

"How to fight, the proper way to use weapons and the ins and outs of his favorite sports—football and basketball," she said and smiled.

Griffin intertwined their hands. "That love you speak of…I'm sure it will come in time. In fact, I think it's already starting to make an appearance. Wouldn't you agree?"

Felicia felt her cheeks turn scarlet and she lowered her head slightly. "Yes, but what about Jia? You were just planning to propose to her."

Griffin pulled his hand free and used the knuckle of his index finger to raise Felicia's chin. "No, my mother was planning on me proposing to Jia. That's over."

"Since when?" She quirked an eyebrow.

"Since you informed me that we share a child. I'm not in love with Jia. She's not the woman I want," Griffin explained.

Felicia shook her head. "No, I didn't want that."

"This is no longer about what either of us wants. It's about what's best for Alyia—and that's to have both of her parents in her life full-time. Will you at least think about it?"

No, she thought but said, "Sure, but I make no promises."

Griffin smiled. "I don't need promises, only compliance," he whispered before plying her with a tamer kiss.

Chapter 18

Felicia was sitting with her back against the headboard, holding one of the hotel's designer pillows to her chest as her mind replayed all the events from the previous night, when her phone began dancing across the nightstand. She double-checked the time on her alarm clock, knowing it was early as the sun was barely breaking through the darkness of the sky. For a moment she was consumed by fear, because the last time she'd received a call this early in the morning from this very number, she was told about her father's heart attack, an attack that had forced his early semiretirement.

"Mom, is everything okay?" she asked, springing forward and tossing the pillow to the side.

Victoria Blake was the girls' mother and go-to person for all things emotional.

"Yes, darling. I just thought we could have a nice chat before both our days get too crazy."

"At seven in the morning?" she asked.

"You're up and so am I," she responded nonchalantly.

"Yes, but how did you know that I would be up?" Felicia asked, sitting back against the headboard.

"A mother knows these things. Do you need a moment to get some coffee or, better yet, tea?"

"No, thank you. I'm fine. Where's Dad, Mom? If you're up, I know he is, too."

Victoria laughed. "He's out for his morning walk. How's our beautiful grandbaby doing?"

"She's wonderful, such a happy child."

"That's all any mother can ask for. Now, how are you? I know you're still trying to get used to all of this…becoming an instant mother and all."

"I really don't know how you did it with three of us at once." Felicia adjusted the pillow behind her. "I know how really fortunate we are to have all these resources at our disposal but that doesn't…"

"But it doesn't help with the uncertainty about your decisions, the fear that you're screwing up and that you could permanently damage your child. A child you love more than your own life. Am I close?" Victoria prompted.

"Close? You nailed it. How did you know? You couldn't have felt that way. You were absolutely the perfect mom," Felicia insisted, her eyes stinging with unshed tears.

Victoria laughed and sighed. "Oh, sweetheart…you really are a dear one, but I was far from perfect. And, yes, we have it financially easier than most, but that doesn't help with the emotional aspect of being a mom, especially a new mom, instantly and unexpectedly, at that."

"Ms. Ellen is great, but I'm afraid Alyia has been, and may have to continue to, spend more time with her than me. My job requires so much time, not to mention all the required travel."

"Remember money brings options. They can go with you wherever you travel. Now, I won't lie…no one can replace the time that a child spends with its mother—"

"That's another thing I'm worried about. Valerie is—was—her mother and I'm just someone she sort of picked to raise her."

"Don't be ridiculous." Victoria's voice rose slightly.

"Blood gives us the physical connection. Love gives us the relationship. When you first returned home with that beautiful angel in your arms, I could see it, the connection…the love. I've seen you interact with Alyia, and your love for each other just shines through. As far as how much time you devote to motherhood? Well, you know how I feel about that. You just have to figure out what works best for you."

"Great, you think I should devote my life to raising her, too? What about the career I've worked so hard for?"

The line went silent for several moments before Victoria said, "Um, I've been here before."

"Excuse me," Felicia said.

"I'm having a déjà vu moment. Look, sweetheart, a lot of women have fulfilling careers and have wonderfully happy home lives, too. You can have both, with or without a partner."

"I was waiting to see how long it would take before you asked about Griffin," Felicia responded, laughing.

"I figured you'll tell us when there's something to tell."

Felicia knew there wasn't much her mother was willing to keep from their father. "Nothing's been settled yet, but Griffin wants for us to raise Alyia together." *That's enough information for now. Anything more would send them both over the edge.*

"Well, that's a great start. Children need both parents in their life. Speaking of which, your father is back. Hold on for a second."

"How was your walk?" Felicia heard her mother ask. After nearly a minute she finally heard her mother say, "Wow, that good?"

Felicia knew that meant her father had just treated her mother to one of his breathtaking, heart-stopping kisses, as her mother described them, that they often shared regardless of who was around.

"Still there, darling?"

"Yes, Mother."

"Stop worrying. Whatever you decide to do will be what's best for both you and Alyia. Now, your father wants to speak to you," she said.

Victoria tried to muffle the phone for a little privacy by covering the receiver, but Felicia still heard her mother say, "If we're going to try to make it to the early morning church service, make this call quick, so *you* don't have to be too quick," she said, giggling. "Otherwise you'll just have to wait until we get back home."

"Eww…"

"How's my baby girl?" Frank Blake, chairman of the board of Blake and Montgomery, asked.

"I was doing fine until Mom's little overshare. She really has to learn how to use the mute button on that expensive phone system we bought you guys for Christmas last year."

"I won't keep you long," he said, his excitement clear.

"I bet," she murmured, shivering.

"What's up with Boy Wonder?"

"We're still working on it. Don't worry. We'll work it out."

"I have no doubt that you will, and if you need me to help him figure things out for you, just let me know."

Felicia laughed. "Yes, sir."

"Now, for a little business." He transitioned.

"Business?" Felicia sat forward with her elbow resting on her leg and her face in her left hand.

"Yes. You haven't attended a board meeting in I don't know how long."

"Yes, but Francine—"

"Francine is not you. She may have your proxy, but you need to make an appearance from time to time. This is your company, too, remember."

Her father's words struck a chord. Felicia's work meant

the world to her, but so did her family. She felt bad about taking the easy way out and giving Francine her proxy. Everyone had made every effort to accommodate her schedule so she could attend the meetings and play a more active role in her family's company. While the majority of the dates were just impossible, there were times that she could have made adjustments.

"Yes, sir." Felicia reached over to cut off the alarm that had just started going off. "I understand and I'll try to do better."

"Good."

"On that note, I'm going to go get in a workout before Alyia wakes up."

"Me, too…" Frank said.

"Gross…"

"Bye, baby girl. Love you."

"Bye, Dad."

Felicia shook her head as she dropped the call. As crazy as she thought her parents were for their tendency to overshare their love life, Felicia had to admit that she was both proud and a little envious of what they had. She could actually envision that type of relationship with Griffin. Felicia smiled at the idea of providing a few uncomfortable moments for their daughter.

She quickly changed into her workout gear, grabbed a bottle of water and headed down to the gym.

Chapter 19

A few hours later Felicia sat cross-legged on the floor with Alyia and watched as she tried to master the art of crawling. When Alyia couldn't make her hands and knees work the way she wanted, she settled for rolling toward her target. In this instance, it was Felicia.

"Almost, baby girl," she cheered.

Felicia's iPad chimed as she reached and brought Alyia up into her arms. "Let's see who's calling us."

Felicia placed her iPad on the coffee table and accepted the incoming video call. She tickled and kissed Alyia as she waited for it to connect.

"There's my beautiful niece," Francine said.

"Well, hello to you, too," Felicia teased the green-eyed reflection of herself.

"Sorry. Hello, sister dear."

"Hi, Felicia. Bye, Felicia," a familiar but out of sight voice said from somewhere behind Francine; he didn't come within the camera's range.

"Hi, Meeks. Where is he?" Felicia asked her sister, trying to see past her through the small screen.

"He's leaving," Francine informed her.

"Let me guess. He's going on a food run," she stated between laughs.

"Alyia, tell your mother to leave your auntie alone."

Both sisters laughed at Alyia's puzzled expression as her gaze darted between her mother and Francine on the screen. "Do you think we confuse her too much when we get together like this?"

"Of course," Felicia said, rubbing her nose against Alyia's cheek. "She'll pick up on the differences soon enough."

"If you say so." Francine sighed and winced as she rubbed her stomach with the palm of her hand.

"How are you doing?" Felicia frowned at the squint in her sister's eyes that signaled the two babies she carried were giving her a hard time.

"I'm doing all right. I just hate having to be on partial bed rest. My babies are fighting for space and I'm ready to evict them with the quickness."

Instant motherhood, though not in the traditional sense, had been an unexpected joy for Felicia. She was thankful every day for the loving relationship she'd developed with Alyia. Yet she couldn't help but wonder what it might have been like to have Griffin's child growing in her belly with him at her side.

Felicia laughed as she rocked from side to side, mimicking Alyia's actions. "You only have a couple more months to go and the longer they stay put, the better."

"I know, Doctor, I know," Francine groaned, bringing a glass of juice to her mouth.

"So what do I owe this call to, or do I need to even ask?"

"No, you don't," Francine said before bringing the glass back to her lips for another sip.

"Okay..."

"So, how did things go last night?" Francine asked before putting a piece of fruit in her mouth. "Did you get Griffin to agree to some type of custody arrangement?"

Felicia knew she'd be hearing from one of her sisters

this morning, but she had expected it to be Farrah. "Things went about how you'd expect and, no, we didn't come to any agreement on custody. However, Griffin did propose marriage."

Francine held the glass midway to her lips. "What?" She blinked several times then placed the glass on the table next to her chair. "He proposed to you?"

"No, I said he proposed that we get married…for Alyia's sake. He wants to give her a proper environment to grow up in with both parents playing active and full-time roles." Felicia placed a fidgeting Alyia back on her toy-filled blanket.

"A marriage of convenience. Why would he want such a thing?" Felicia's gaze left the screen for a moment. "What *aren't* you saying?"

Felicia knew she wouldn't be able to keep this from her sister. "There wouldn't be anything convenient about that marriage at all."

"Wait, are you saying he wants a real marriage? With sex and everything?" Francine stopped rocking in her chair. A mixture of curiosity and excitement was coming through loud and clear.

Griffin's kiss popped into Felicia's mind. The way he'd held her in his arms, caressed her face, ran his tongue across her lips… She released a deep sigh.

"Felicia. Felicia!" Francine yelled.

"What?"

"Yes, 'what'?" Francine's eyes narrowed. "Did you—?"

"Of course not," she replied, and couldn't help the color that flamed her face. "We just kissed."

Francine laughed. "Must've been some kiss."

"Knock, knock…excuse me," Ms. Ellen said as she entered the room holding a small cup and spoon. "It's time for this little one's midmorning snack. Is it all right if I take her?"

Alyia squealed in delight at the sight of what Ms. Ellen held in her hand. "Looks like it," Felicia said, laughing.

"Hello, Ms. Francine," Ms. Ellen said, smiling and waving at the screen. "How you feeling?"

"Big. Huge, actually," she replied, rubbing her stomach to illustrate her point. "Thanks for asking."

Ms. Ellen laughed. "Well, you look lovely." She reached down and scooped up a bouncing Alyia. "Ready for some applesauce?"

"See you later, sweetie." Felicia kissed Alyia on the cheek before whispering in her ear, "Mommy loves you."

"Bye, Auntie's baby," Francine called after them. "You couldn't be a better mother if you'd given birth to her."

"Thanks, sis," she whispered, warmed by the compliment.

"Now, what's really going on with you?" Francine asked.

"Nothing's going on," she said in a low tone, reflecting on the last exchange. "It was just a kiss and I have no intention of marrying Griffin or anyone else unless I'm in love."

"Looks to me like you're halfway there now," Francine teased.

"I. Am. Not...sure what I am." Felicia felt the heat rise from her neck and continue upward, but she refused to drop her eyes. That would certainly give away more than she intended.

"You're definitely *in like* or something. Your face lights up just talking about him. That kiss you were 'thinking' about got me excited." She used her right hand to fan herself, then playfully looked over her shoulder. "Where *is* my husband when I need him?"

Felicia ignored her sister's amusement at her expense. "Okay, I'll own up that I might have more than just friendly feelings for Griffin, but I'm still not marrying him."

"Good," she said, brushing a wayward curl from her

face. "So what are you going to do now that you'll be accepting that promotion?"

"How do you know?" she said, paused and added, "Never mind. I still haven't completely made up my mind."

Francine adjusted the pillow behind her back. "You will. Your career, your research, is a big part of who you are. This promotion is just too good not to accept."

"You're right. Medical biochemistry addresses the causes of cancer and a host of other genetic diseases, not to mention the thousands of biochemical weapons that get created every day." Felicia had had a single focus ever since she'd accepted the position at the CIA, and that had been to protect her country at all costs.

Felicia's smile widened. "Just think, I'll be heading a group of brilliant-minded people in this newly developed... what?" Felicia asked, watching Francine's mouth curve into a big smile. "What is it? Are you all right?"

"I'm fine. I'm just so very proud of you. You're so passionate about your work and I rarely get to see that side of you, is all."

"I am passionate about my work, but I'm more passionate about being a good mother to Alyia. I just have to figure out a way to balance it all."

"You will, sweetie." Francine leaned back in her chair, laughing. "Now that you've skillfully distracted me, back to my question. What are you going to do about Griffin?"

Felicia brought her knees to her chest and wrapped her arms around them. "I have an idea, but I don't think you're going to like it."

Chapter 20

Felicia pulled her new red Mercedes-AMG CLA, another welcome-home gift from her sisters, into the hospital parking lot; she was meeting Griffin for lunch.

Felicia came alive walking the halls of Grady Memorial Hospital, the largest in the state of Georgia. Felicia might not be on staff, wearing her scrubs and stethoscope or working in a subpar facility on the other side of the world, but the white walls and sparkling floors made her feel right at home. The hustle and bustle of doctors and nurses trying to care for their patients, especially on a Monday morning, was a welcome and familiar sight.

"Dr. Blake?"

Felicia looked back in the direction from which her name had been called. "Yes?"

"Dr. Blake, I'm Dr. Trent Green, chief of staff," said a tall man with ivory skin and muscles everywhere. "Welcome to Grady Memorial."

Felicia quickly racked her brain, trying to place where she might have met this man, built like a bodybuilder in training. Before she could fill in the blanks, the mystery was solved.

"We haven't met," he explained. "But I've followed your work in biochemistry."

Felicia's forehead creased. She wasn't sure how that was possible since most of what she did for the CIA was classified. But once again, before she could question him about what he thought he knew, he clarified his point. "Your published work on safer options for chemically treating cancer cells is revolutionary."

Oh, that work, she thought with a relieved sigh. "Thank you. I work with a great group of people."

"Beautiful and modest," he said, gifting her with a sexy smile that would probably draw in some women, but not her.

"Good afternoon, Dr. Green," a pretty blond nurse said as she passed them in the hallway. The good doctor acknowledged the young nurse with a nod and sly smile that confirmed Felicia's suspicions that he was a bit of a hound.

"So what brings you to Grady? You can't possibly be sick," he continued, his eyes sweeping her body before returning to her face.

"Thank you. And, no, I'm not sick. Actually, I'm here to meet a friend for lunch." In that moment Trent Green's flirtatious disposition disappeared. A deep frown marred his face. He was looking past Felicia at something behind her. She immediately felt a hand gently touch the small of her back. She looked up to see a tight-jawed Griffin and Trent Green scowling at each other.

"Anything I can do for you, Dr. Kaile?" Green asked through an obviously forced smile.

"Not a single thing, Dr. Green," Griffin replied, his tone taking on a deep, harsh tone that Felicia had never heard before.

"I assume you two know each other." Trent Green's eyes darted from Felicia to Griffin.

"You assume correctly." Griffin smiled down at Felicia, who frowned, thinking, *Enough of this macho bull*.

"Griffin and I are old friends. We went to medical

school together," Felicia offered right before Griffin's hand slid down her back slightly and her breath caught in her throat.

"We should go," Griffin said in a husky tone that was more suggestive than it should have been. "We don't want to be late for our reservation."

"Should we expect to see you at this afternoon's staff meeting?" Trent asked with one raised eyebrow.

"Have I ever missed a meeting, Dr. Green?" he replied.

Trent matched his move and said, "There's a first time for everything."

Felicia reached for Griffin's hand and intertwined their fingers. His shoulders lowered slightly. "We should go. It was nice meeting you, Dr. Green."

"It was my pleasure, Dr. Blake," he said in a tone that was as husky and suggestive as Griffin's had been a few moments earlier. "I'm sure we'll be seeing each other again soon." Trent gave Griffin a small smirk before turning to leave. He pulled out his phone as he made his way down the hall.

Standing there, holding Griffin's hand, trying to keep him calm, was having the opposite effect on her body. Felicia pulled her hand free, turned to face Griffin and poked her index finger in his chest. "What was that all about?" she demanded.

"Nothing. We better go. We don't want to miss our reservation." Griffin led her down the hall and out to his waiting car. He opened the door to a black Porsche Sienna and helped Felicia inside.

Griffin came around the car and slid in behind the wheel. "I think you're going to like this place. They serve some of the best Thai food in the city," he said. "You still like Thai, right?"

"Of course, but I can't believe you remembered that. We only had it once."

"Yes, but it was an adventure that was too hard to forget." Griffin smiled and made his eyebrows dance, causing her to giggle.

After driving a few blocks they were wheeling into the driveway of a small restaurant with a packed parking lot. Griffin parked, cut the engine and looked over to her. "Do you remember that night?"

Felicia smiled. "After we finished our last final, Val wanted Thai and Todd said he knew of this great restaurant…but then we got lost trying to find the place."

"And we ended up in the middle of nowhere, where we ran out of gas," Griffin added.

Felicia nodded. "We eventually found the place and it ended up being in some sketchy-looking building, but it had been the best Thai I had ever eaten. Too bad they didn't take credit cards," Felicia said.

"Yeah, and we'd spent all the cash we had getting Todd's truck towed to that gas station," he said, laughing.

"The four of us spent the night working off our meal."

Felicia smiled, only to be hit by a sharp pain in her heart, remembering Valerie's betrayal. Her smile disappeared.

"It was one of the most fun nights I'd had in a long time," he said, suddenly sounding very serious as he stared into her eyes. "Or since."

"Me, too," she said, holding his gaze.

Griffin leaned over and cupped Felicia's face with his right hand, running his thumb over her lips before kissing her gently. He leaned his forehead against hers. "We can make this work for all of us."

"Griffin—"

"We'd better get inside. I may have exaggerated about the need for a reservation, but it does get pretty crowded. And we wouldn't want anyone tapping on the window because we've been sitting in the car too long."

Felicia checked her watch. "Will you have enough time? You do have a meeting to get back to," she said sarcastically, remembering that unnecessary little altercation back at the hospital.

Griffin smirked, unfazed by her chastisement. "I'll be just fine. I ordered already. They know me here."

"Of course you did."

"I hope you don't mind," he said with a sheepish grin. "I think I remembered what you liked."

Felicia bit her lip but quickly released it. "I guess we better get inside, then."

Griffin quickly exited the car and came around to open Felicia's door. He held her hand as they entered the restaurant. Griffin greeted the hostess in Thai, as did Felicia. Griffin's head snapped down to Felicia, gray eyes sparkling with excitement. "You speak Thai? I knew you spoke Mandarin, but Thai, too. Impressive."

"Not fluently," she admitted. "I've always been good at picking up different languages and it comes in handy with all my travels for work."

"If you'll follow me, your table is ready," the young lady said, heading toward the back of the restaurant.

Griffin and Felicia made their way through the restaurant when they came upon two couples. "Hello, Mother, Father," Griffin greeted them. Then, to the others seated at the table, he said, "Mr. and Mrs. Richardson."

Chapter 21

Griffin's grip on Felicia's hand tightened as she tried—and failed—to free herself from his hold. "This is a nice surprise," he said, leaning forward and kissing his mother on the cheek. His father stood and Griffin gave him a one-armed hug. "Nice to see you again, Mr. and Mrs. Richardson," he said, offering them a quick nod. "Everyone, allow me to introduce my—"

"Felicia Blake," she said, successfully pulling her hand free and putting some distance between them.

"It's nice to see you again, Felicia," Griffin's father said, pulling Felicia into an embrace. "I hear you're doing some really big things to keep our country safe."

"I'm trying," Felicia reassured, stepping out of his hold.

Lin Kaile offered Felicia a half smile that was as forced as she remembered, but the woman remained silent.

"Ms. Blake, it's a pleasure to meet you," Mr. Richardson said, giving Felicia a tight smile; Mrs. Richardson continued to stare, her face void of expression, but she didn't offer any greeting whatsoever.

"It's Dr. Blake, actually," Griffin told him.

"Forgive me... Dr. Blake," Mr. Richardson corrected.

Felicia nudged Griffin in the side for him to lay off but said, "No problem."

"We won't hold you up. Please enjoy your lunch." Griffin gestured toward the four bowls of food sitting in front of them.

They followed the waitress who was waiting by a closed bar to escort them to a small section at the back of the restaurant that, thankfully, was several tables away from Griffin's parents.

"That was awkward."

"Sorry about that," Griffin said, pulling out Felicia's chair.

He settled her into a spot with her back to the small group. "I'm sure it's about to get even more so. If I know my mother, Jia will be showing up at any moment."

"What?" Felicia's hand froze for a moment before she continued to place her napkin across her lap.

"It's my mother's way of plotting to get us back together, I'm sure," Griffin explained.

"How would she even know we'd be here?"

"The same way she knows everything." Griffin placed his napkin in his lap and his keys and phone on the table. "She has sources at the hospital that would gladly tell her my schedule. My assistant can't seem to keep her mouth shut when it comes to my mother."

"I'm sure your mother can be a very convincing woman when she wants to be."

"That she can, but I'm her boss. Her loyalty should be to me."

Felicia nodded. "Maybe you should gently remind her of that fact again."

"Or just have her switched to another department and hire someone from outside who will be more amenable to keeping my business to themselves.

"Felicia, would you rather go someplace else?" he asked, handing her the drink menu.

"No, we're just two old friends having lunch," she said, scanning the list of teas the restaurant offered.

"Hardly." Griffin picked up his own drink menu. "I don't hold hands with women that I'm *just friends* with."

Felicia lowered her menu. "What's with this territorial act you have going on right now? First with Dr. Green and now in front of your parents."

Griffin placed his menu to the side. "This isn't an act. You and Alyia are my family and I'm more than ready to claim you both."

"First of all, *Alyia* is your family," she corrected. "I'm just someone you knew a long time ago and now we happen to share responsibility for raising a child. That's all."

"Bull!" he shot back. "We're more than that and you know it."

Felicia continued, ignoring his statement. "Second, that scene at the hospital had nothing to do with Alyia. So what gives?"

Before Griffin could offer his explanation, the waitress came to take their drink order and confirm the preordered chicken and rice special Griffin had placed earlier. Once their order had been taken, Felicia sat back in her chair with her hands placed in her lap. "Well?"

Griffin smirked. "Trent and I have some type of love-hate relationship going on. We love and respect the work that we do, but can't stand each other on a personal level."

"You're both successful in two completely different fields. This animosity can't be professional."

Griffin lifted his left eyebrow. "I never said that it was."

"So it *is* personal. Let me guess, a woman." Felicia sat back and folded her arms. "Who did the stealing?"

"Neither. They were long over before we started dating."

Felicia dropped her arms and leaned forward. "Jia?"

Griffin's brows drew together. "No…Kathy."

Felicia's mouth opened then quickly closed.

"Like I said, they were over before I asked her out, but apparently her preference for me rubbed him the wrong way."

"I can imagine." Felicia's phone rang and she reached into her purse to retrieve it. She looked at the screen and answered, "Dr. Blake." Felicia stood, raised her index finger and excused herself to take the call in private.

Griffin was so busy watching Felicia walk away that he hadn't noticed his mother approaching the table. "Griffin…"

Griffin looked heavenward and sighed before standing to greet her. "Yes, Mother."

Lin took the seat abandoned by Felicia. "What's going on with you and that girl?"

He was taken aback by her caustic tone. "I love you, Mother, but that's really none of your business."

Lin flinched, her eyes fluttered with a flash he recognized as annoyance. "Remember who you're speaking to," she warned in Mandarin.

Griffin offered one nod, his jaw set. "My relationship with Felicia isn't something I'm ready to discuss with you yet," he replied in her native language.

"Relationship," she scoffed, turning her nose as though she smelled something rotten. "You barely know that woman."

"I know her better than you think."

Lin smirked. "A sexual attraction doesn't make a relationship. She can never be a wife and mother. Not the one you need. She's a high-powered career woman and she'll never give that up for you."

"And I'd never ask her to. But you'd be surprised what she's capable of being." Griffin's confidence in Felicia even surprised him.

Felicia returned to the table. "Mrs. Kaile, hello again."

Lin pursed her lips and didn't utter a word.

Felicia turned her attention to Griffin as he stood.

"My apologies, but duty calls." She gestured with her phone.

"No problem," he said, trying to tamp down his disappointment. "I'll just take care of the check."

"No, that won't be necessary. Please stay and enjoy lunch with your family." Felicia smiled at Lin, who grimaced her displeasure. "They've sent a car for me," Felicia explained.

"What? Who?"

Felicia shrugged. "It can't be helped."

"Who?" he asked again.

Felicia looked at him, trying to get a message across that he couldn't fathom.

"Please excuse us, Mother." Griffin pulled Felicia to the side. "What's going on?"

"I have to go," she answered, her mouth forming a half smile.

"I get that, but like this? I can take you wherever you need to go," he said. "We have to talk. Decisions must be made."

"I understand that, but this is my job—"

"Excuse me, Dr. Blake," said a tall man wearing a black suit.

Felicia held up her right hand. "Just one minute." She turned back to Griffin. "That's my ride."

"Let's have dinner tonight," he asked, trying to keep the frustration out of his voice. Why did it seem life was throwing them together and then putting obstacles in their path just for fun?

"I'm not sure when I'll be done, but feel free to go by the hotel and see Alyia."

"I will." Griffin pulled Felicia into his arms and gave her an overpowering kiss on the lips. "Call me later."

"We'll talk, I promise," she said before gathering her things and turning to leave. "Goodbye, Mrs. Kaile."

When his mother didn't respond, Felicia peered at her and repeated her farewell, this time in Mandarin.

Lin Kaile's eyes flashed with the type of blaze a fire department would consider to be multiple alarms' worth. The moment Felicia was out of earshot, she snarled, "Nope, I'm not at all surprised at what that woman is capable of." She then straightened her hardened expression, affecting a more admissible one instead. "Now come join us for lunch, darling. Jia should be here any minute."

Griffin gave his head a slow shake and checked his watch. "Actually, Mother, I have a meeting to get to."

"Don't be rude to our guests," she snapped.

"I'm being no ruder to your guests than you were to mine," he quipped. "I have to go."

"But, son—"

Griffin kissed her cheek then walked past and gave a small wave to his father, who nodded, and one to the Richardsons, who frowned. Then he lightly touched Jia, who had just entered the restaurant, on the shoulder as a goodbye.

"You're leaving?" she asked with a look to him and then a shocked glance at his mother.

"Indeed," he replied with a look over his shoulder at his mother's crestfallen expression before leaving the restaurant.

Chapter 22

Griffin walked into the large auditorium-style classroom where the afternoon staff meeting was being held. He stood next to the door since it was the only space available in the hundred-plus-seat room, which was nearly filled to capacity with people from multiple medical disciplines and other staff.

"Wow, something deep must be up," declared Ida Jones, the mahogany-skinned, petite, fifty-year-old director of nursing. She slid into the spot next to Griffin, her brown eyes scanning the room and glossed lips pulling into a pout. "What's going on?"

"I have no idea," he whispered, wondering if this meeting somehow had anything to do with why Felicia had been called away so suddenly. "I was expecting our regular boring staff meeting."

"Hardly, not after the CDC invaded the emergency room."

"What? When?" Griffin's forehead creased.

"Fifteen minutes ago. Where have *you* been?" She squinted, giving him a once-over as though his eyes, smile and overall demeanor would tell her something he wouldn't voice out loud.

"Lunch…"

"Well, aren't you special, going out to lunch on a Monday," she said.

"Good afternoon, everyone," Dr. Trent Green said, speaking into a wireless microphone as he entered the room. It looked more like a no-questions-asked press conference than the normal staff meeting Griffin was used to. Four doctors filed in behind the chief of staff, one of whom Griffin knew very well. Her presence confirmed his thinking.

"I won't keep you long," Trent said to the attentive crowd. "But we have a situation in the hospital that I have to bring everyone up to speed on. We have identified two patients with Legionnaires' disease, the same bacterial strain as in New York, but we have a team working to confirm."

The room broke out in a low murmur of conversation but Griffin kept his eyes on the striking doctor standing next to Trent Green, the one who was trying not to meet his gaze.

"Please, folks, settle down," Green said. "We'll try to answer your questions with statements from our specialists." He gestured to the people who were now on either side of him. "First up, CDC Director Dr. Stacy Gray." Trent handed her the microphone.

"Good afternoon, ladies and gentlemen. As you know, the CDC is responsible for addressing any medical outbreaks that occur on a state or global level. Our presence today is based solely on the disease that brought us here and nothing that any of you may or may not have done." Stacy Gray's eyes scanned the room as though assessing the relief associated with that statement. "Let me introduce the team responsible for helping us get through this situation. Dr. Carl Jeff, Associate Director of Science, Carmen Morris, my chief of staff, and Dr. Felicia Blake, a biochemistry expert on loan from the CIA. With that said, I'd like Dr. Jeff to give you an update on what we know so far."

Griffin tried to pay attention to what the good doctor was saying, but all he could think about was what role Felicia could possibly play. Her brilliant mind and ability to run a medical team full of different specialties so effortlessly would be a tremendous asset to any hospital. Griffin was struggling to stay forced on her mental capabilities because he wanted her so badly. He loved how sweet her mouth tasted. The way their tongues danced, how good her body felt in his arms. Griffin began to imagine what else she could do with that beautiful mouth of hers and his body began to respond to the idea when he felt a nudge at his side.

"Griffin," Ida said, nudging him again.

"What?" he asked, meeting her eyes, embarrassed that he let his thoughts get out of control when he clearly needed to focus on the biological breakdown of the disease, treatment and care plan options that could provide resolutions not only for their area but for the country. Griffin was fighting with the idea of how something this dangerous could land in his own backyard. And though he understood it was Felicia's job to find answers to those types of questions, he was very grateful that her role was limited to the medical and scientific ends of things and not the criminal aspect. That area would put her right in the line of fire when it comes to chasing down and capturing the responsible parties.

"You didn't fall asleep standing up, now, did you?" she whispered, a tinge of humor in her voice.

"Of course not."

"Good. I'm sure you don't want to miss hearing from the woman you've been staring at since she hit the door," she said with a low chuckle.

Griffin's eyes darted to Felicia, who was being handed

the microphone. "Good afternoon, everyone. I'm Dr. Blake."

Murmurs of curiosity made their way through the audience.

"What we know for sure is that both senior patients are not residents of New York, nor have they traveled outside the state of Georgia within the last six months. Neither of them have any idea how they could have contracted the disease." Felicia walked to the right side of the room to ensure that they, too, could hear and understand her. "As you know, this disease doesn't spread from person to person and has to be administered through a coolant system. We are in the process of trying to determine where these patients could've inhaled the mist, contracting this disease."

Felicia made her way to the other side of the room, near Griffin, who was leaning against the wall. "We have teams in place, scouring the city, trying to determine the point of initial contact," she continued after a brief pause when recognition dawned in her eyes. "Finding that location will help us answer many questions that I can't answer at this time."

Felicia handed the microphone back to Stacy Gray and took a step back before her eyes found Griffin, who gave her a tiny wave of acknowledgment.

It was late afternoon when Felicia exited the elevator onto a secure floor, where she had to announce herself to the person monitoring the camera and wait to be escorted to her destination.

"Dr. Blake, welcome to the CDC. I'm Dr. Samantha Raymond," a pretty blond woman wearing blue scrubs and a white lab coat said, offering her hand. "Dr. Gray assigned me to assist you."

"Thank you," Felicia said, shaking the woman's hand.

"I hate I couldn't get here any earlier but it's been a crazy start to the week."

Between Griffin's proposal and pretending that his mother trying to push him toward Jia at lunch didn't bother her, Felicia couldn't wait to focus on something else for a little while.

"This way," Samantha directed.

They walked down a long, desolate hallway, passing several doors before they finally stopped in front of a large sliding door with a security pad on the wall next to it. Samantha waved a key card in front of it and the door slid open. Felicia followed the woman into a dark room.

"Dr. Gray thought you'd like an office with easy access to the lab. Just go through that door," she explained, pointing to the far left corner. "It leads right into the lab."

"That's great, thank you."

Samantha nodded. "Where would you like to start?"

Felicia dropped her bag on the desk and walked over to the small conference table where stacks of legal pads, pens and two electronic tablets sat. She had everything she needed, including two large dry-erase boards that had been set up.

Samantha joined her at the table.

"Let's break down the groups of infected patients," she said, sifting through the documents that had a watermark signaling they had come from the FBI. "Our primary objective is to determine where they had been within twenty-four hours of becoming sick."

"Yes, ma'am."

They would be working closely and often late, and formality wouldn't factor in. "It's Felicia, please."

"Yes, Felicia."

Felicia moved over to the whiteboard, where she wrote *New York senior center, California San Quentin State prison, Chicago senior center, Atlanta HIV support group.*

"These are all the current locations where we believe the patients could have been infected. Let's see if we can confirm that and figure out how they all got sick."

Samantha reached for the tablets and fired them up. "All the patient records are here. The CIA, FBI and the hospital did a complete history and full assessment on each patient." Samantha handed Felicia one of the tablets.

"Excellent. Let's get to work."

"Ms. Ellen, you sure this is okay?" Griffin asked, his left hand gingerly supporting Alyia's back while he bathed her with his right.

Griffin had very skilled hands and was a master under pressure in the operating room, but holding his daughter while she laughed and wiggled made him extremely nervous. His heart overflowed with love for his beautiful Alyia, yet he felt ill-prepared as a father. He still had a lot to learn.

"Of course. See how she's splashing and giggling? Alyia knows she's making a mess and that her daddy doesn't mind. She's enjoying all those surprised faces you're making whenever she pushes the water on you," she said, laughing.

"When Felicia suggested I come have dinner with Alyia, I didn't realize I would have the opportunity to share bath time responsibilities. Thank you," he said, keeping his eyes on Alyia.

"Anytime. She *is* your daughter," she lovingly reminded.

"I can't get over how much her eyes are like mine." Griffin kissed Alyia on her wet head. "You think she's good now?"

"I do. Here's her towel."

"Thank you." Griffin tossed it across his shoulder before picking Alyia up out of the water. He quickly wrapped a cooing Alyia in the large towel monogrammed with an *A* and carried her to the changing table.

"Everything you need is on that first shelf—lotion, powder, diapers and her nightclothes."

Griffin took extra care drying and dressing Alyia, laughing at her attempts to bring her feet to her mouth. "Are you hungry, my sweet girl?"

"Well, it is about that time," Ms. Ellen offered, walking toward Griffin with a bottle in hand. "Here you go, Dad."

"Oh, you want me…okay." Griffin sat in the rocking chair, adjusted Alyia in his arms and watched in awe as Alyia held and consumed her bottle. "There's only one more thing that could make this moment perfect."

Ms. Ellen patted Griffin on the shoulder. "She'll be home soon," she said before making her exit.

Griffin looked down at Alyia and said, "Home…"

It was after midnight when Felicia walked into her dimly lit hotel suite and dropped her purse, keys and cell phone on the bar.

"Man, it's been a long day," she whispered as she pulled the rubber band from her hair, freeing the curls that Griffin swore up and down he loved so much. She walked into the kitchen and retrieved a bottle of Chardonnay from the refrigerator. She was pulling a glass from the cabinet when she heard, "Care to share?"

Griffin stepped out of the shadows.

Felicia nearly dropped the glass as she inhaled a sharp intake of breath. "Dammit, Griffin, you scared the hell out of me." She released that breath slowly. "It's midnight. What are you doing here?"

"Sorry. I came to have dinner with Alyia, ended up bathing her, too, and I decided to wait for you. Ms. Ellen thought it would be fine. I guess I dozed off."

Felicia reached for another glass and filled them both.

She handed him one and took several sips from her own. "I'm sorry I couldn't tell you why I had to cut out at lunch. That's just how it is at times."

"I get it. I don't like it, but I get it." Griffin took a sip of his wine.

"So why did you wait?"

"So we could talk, settle things. Today's a great example as to why we should get married."

"How's that?" Felicia took another sip of her wine.

"Alyia should be with one of her parents at all times."

"We don't have to be married for that," she countered. "Besides, Ms. Ellen has been her nanny all of her life."

"Ms. Ellen is wonderful, but she's not her parent. Together we can make sure one of us is always available."

"We're both busy doctors. There may be times when neither of us can be available," she reminded him. "Which is why we need Ms. Ellen."

"I agree, but as partners we can ensure that those times are rare," he said.

Felicia placed the glass on the bar and peered at him, wondering at his sudden push for marriage and trying to get a line on where his mind was heading. "I agree, being together is ideal but, like I said, we don't have to be married for that."

"Of course we do." There was an edge of disbelief in his voice. "You can't deny that we care for each other," he said, staring into her eyes. "How else do you suggest we accomplish it?"

She drained her wineglass before she spoke. "We can start by simply sharing accommodations."

"Living together?" Griffin frowned.

"Yes, we can share parenting duties while really getting to know each other again."

Griffin's forehead relaxed and he put his glass down

next to hers. "Are you committed to trying to really make this work?"

"I sure am," she replied. "I love Alyia."

He grimaced and added, "I mean, to seeing where things could lead between the two of us?"

"Now, that's something totally dif—"

"Stop talking," Griffin commanded, cupping her face with both hands and devouring her lips. Within moments his left hand was buried in her hair and he was backing Felicia up against the wall of the kitchenette. Griffin raised his head and stared into her eyes.

"I know it sounds crazy but…I missed you," he whispered.

"I…missed you…too," she said between breaths.

Griffin kissed Felicia again, only with more reverence this time. His right hand made its way under her scrub top where he unhooked her bra's front clasp. Griffin sucked Felicia's tongue as his hands played with her nipples.

"Oh, my, that feels so good," Felicia cried. "I want… I…"

Griffin removed Felicia's top, kissing and licking her neck, collarbone and the valley of her breasts before taking her nipples in his mouth. His right hand made its way inside her scrub pants and under her panties, where he massaged her sex. Griffin looked into Felicia's face and enjoyed the way her pupils dilated and her lips quivered with each stroke of his hand.

"Oh, Griff… Griffin…"

"Damn, baby, I need a taste." Before Felicia could say otherwise, Griffin dropped to his knees. He lowered her pants and underwear, freed her right leg and placed it over his shoulder. He gripped Felicia's butt with both hands, holding her in place as he parted the soft folds of flesh and kissed her core. Griffin licked and sucked until he heard

Felicia's muffled screams. He kissed his way back up her body, leaving his mark on both of her breasts.

Felicia stood, shaking, while using both hands to cover her mouth keeping in the sounds of her whimpers. Griffin removed her hands and kissed her. "Oh, Griffin," she whispered as tears fell from her eyes. "I…need…more…"

"I know, baby. Me, too," Griffin said, his voice husky. He swept Felicia up into his arms and headed down the hall. "Which one?"

"Last door on the left," she responded between Griffin's kisses.

Griffin placed Felicia on the edge of her bed. "You are so beautiful." Griffin ran the back of his right hand down the side of her face, his thumb paying special attention to her lips. "I know we haven't had a chance to discuss this yet, but don't worry, baby, I'm healthy and I have condoms."

"Good to know. I'm healthy, too, and I'm on the pill," she shared, staring up at him. Felicia couldn't believe she was actually sitting with her body so exposed and she didn't feel in the least bit uncomfortable with Griffin.

"You have no idea how long I've waited for this moment." Griffin began running his hands through her hair.

"Right back at you," she whispered, barely recognizing her own voice. "In fact, I think I should tell you how long I waited."

Griffin got down on his knees in front of Felicia and kissed her gently on the lips, her jaw and neck. Felicia didn't think he'd heard her, so this time she would take her sister's advice. "Griffin," she whispered.

"Yes, baby," he replied, his voice barely above a whisper.

"I have an intact hymen."

Chapter 23

"Wait! Say that again," Farrah said, laughing, leaning back on the sofa in the family room of Griffin's house.

"Stop it, Farrah," Francine ordered, rubbing her stomach.

"Yes, I told the man that I had an intact hymen," Felicia confirmed, covering her face with both hands and shaking her head.

"And you used those exact words, too?" Farrah asked, not even trying to hide her amusement.

Felicia dropped her hands. "Did you two fly all the way here just to give me a hard time?" she asked the blue-and-green-eyed versions of herself.

Francine raised her hand from the expanding belly and reached over to squeeze Felicia's forearm. "Of course not, sweetie, especially since I won't be able to fly after another week."

"Speak for yourself," Farrah teased, winking at Francine.

Francine's eyes flickered with disappointment, causing Farrah to rein herself in and release a small sigh. "Kidding. Now, did you actually think you could call and tell us two days ago that you'd checked out of the hotel, took

Ms. Ellen and our niece and moved in with your baby's daddy, and we'd just let that go?" Farrah asked.

"You want to tell us what happened?" Francine asked.

Felicia brought her knees to her chest and wrapped her arms around her legs, bracing herself as she offered her sisters a replay…

Griffin raised his head slowly, scanning Felicia's face before holding her gaze for a long length of time. "Are you telling me you're a virgin?"

She tensed, worried about his response. "Yes," she whispered.

Griffin reached for the silk robe lying on the chair across from Felicia's bed. He sat next to Felicia on the bed and handed her the garment. "Here, please put this on or I won't be able to concentrate."

A flush crept up Felicia's face as she put her hands through the robe's sleeves and tightened the belt. "Okay."

"Now, how is that even possible?"

"We both know how it's possible." Felicia acknowledged with a nod, "But if you must hear me say it, I've never had sex before."

"Why? I mean…" He turned his body toward hers. "You're the most exquisite woman I've ever met—mind and body. How could any man…? Unless…"

"Unless what?" Felicia asked, frowning. "Finish your thought."

"Did something happen to you?" he asked, his forehead creased and jaw clenched.

Felicia cupped Griffin's face. "No, nothing happened to me." Griffin's relief was unmistakable. "It just never happened for me."

"Why?" Griffin held her hand to his face.

Felicia shrugged and dropped her hand. "Too busy, I guess. It wasn't a priority when I was an undergrad. And medical school... Let's just say things never turned out the way I'd hoped."

Their eyes met and Griffin took Felicia's hand in his. "Well, that's about to change."

"I most certainly hope so," she murmured, flickering a gaze to take in their unkempt state.

"But not tonight."

"Oh." Felicia lowered her eyes.

Griffin lowered his head to gaze into Felicia's eyes. "I want you desperately," Griffin reassured her in the softest tone before pulling Felicia onto his lap, ensuring that she felt the evidence of that fact. "But I also want your first time—our first time together to be special."

Felicia could see the sincerity in Griffin's eyes, making her disappointment a bit more bearable.

"Please say you understand," he said.

Felicia pushed out a long, slow breath. "I understand."

Griffin kissed Felicia gently on the lips. "I'll send a moving company to help pack up your things." Griffin reached into his pocket and pulled out a set of keys and a card with his security information on it. "Here's two sets of keys to the house. One for you and one for Ms. Ellen, along with the alarm code."

"We don't need—"

"We both know that's not true. I've never seen so many toys and devices necessary to raise one small child," Griffin said, smiling.

Felicia laughed. "Yes, Alyia does have a lot of stuff. Most of which you can thank my family for." She looked down at the keys. "You sure you're okay with this? How's your mother going to take it?"

"You're moving into my house...not hers. You let me worry about my mother." Griffin stood. "I'd better get out of here so you can get some rest. We both have a busy few days ahead of us, not to mention this weekend's ball."

"What ball?" she asked standing and adjusting her robe.

Griffin held Felicia's hand as they walked to the door. "My family's annual charity ball. It's Saturday night. It's a little ostentatious, but it benefits a number of worthy causes."

"Me... I... I can't—"

Griffin silenced her with a heart-piercing kiss. "Yes, you can. We're together now, remember."

"Roommates," she corrected.

"No, a couple. You promised you'd see where this could go," Griffin reminded Felicia.

"Yes, but I didn't think it would be to a charity ball... in five days."

Griffin laughed. He kissed her on the corner of her lips and whispered, "Sleep well."

"Right..."

Francine sat with her eyes closed, fanning herself. "Wow..."

"You okay?" Farrah and Felicia asked Francine in unison.

A slow smile spread across her face. "Don't you feel that?" Francine asked Farrah.

Farrah shrugged. "It's just their heat. I guess my own desire for Robert overrides anything they can come up with."

"What?" Felicia asked no one in particular, her eyes wide as saucers.

"Our triplet connection, remember," Francine reminded her.

Felicia giggled. "Sorry, sis."

"How long of a cold shower *did* you have to take?" Farrah smirked.

Felicia couldn't contain her laughter. She remembered

thinking that she'd never get that damn water cold enough.
"A minute...or two."

"Then you just let him pack you up and move you into
his house." Farrah examined the room with a quick sweep
of her intuitive eye. "Which *is* magnificent, by the way,
although it could use a woman's touch."

While Griffin's first floor was pure luxury living, the
second-floor family room screamed "man cave." From
its dark wood floors covered with warm-colored Oriental rugs and a brown leather sectional sofa with an extra-
long day bed attached, to the full entertainment center that
housed an eighty-inch television—all acted as a backdrop
to the wall of windows with its own balcony overlooking
the Olympic-size pool and outside living area with a full
outdoor kitchen.

Felicia nodded. "It is a beautiful house. I still can't believe you two are here," she said, smiling at her sisters.

"It was either us or our parents," Francine added.

"Speaking of which, when do you plan to tell them
you've taken their granddaughter and moved in with a
man they barely know?" Farrah asked.

Felicia raised her shoulders and her face contorted. "I
figure I'd let things settle down a bit, then invite them to
meet everyone."

"Even the mother-in-law from hell?" Farrah asked,
frowning. "How did she take the news, anyway?"

"I don't know. Griffin hasn't told her yet. He was waiting for us to determine how we wanted to handle things.
I'm sure as soon as she finds out she'll start trying to figure out how to get me out of the way."

"Not going to happen," Farrah proclaimed with an ef-
fortless confidence Felicia had come to rely on.

"I'm not worried. Besides, Griffin will make his inten-
tions clear when he tells her about me and Alyia."

"Well, you better make Dad and Mom meeting everyone

a priority," Francine said, attempting to reaching for a glass of tea but finding such a simple task difficult. "Speaking of meeting the family, when am I going to have the pleasure?"

"I got it," Farrah said, handing Francine the glass. "Where is the Boy Wonder, anyway?"

"Thanks." Francine accepted the glass and took a sip.

"He's working," Felicia said.

"Call him. See if he can join us. I didn't come all this way not to lay eyes on the man himself." Francine took a sip of her tea.

Farrah reached in her purse and held out her phone to her sister. "Need my phone?"

"No, I do not, thank you," she said, annoyed by Farrah's sarcastic attitude. Felicia picked up her phone off the coffee table and dialed Griffin.

"Hey, baby," Griffin answered.

"Hi. Look, my sisters are in town—"

"Both of them?"

Felicia giggled. "Yes, and they *really* want to meet you. Francine, anyway. You think you could break away for a while?"

"I'll move a few things around. See you in a bit," he said before ending the call.

"He'll be here shortly," Felicia announced, placing her phone back on the table.

"Good. Now, where was I? You know how Dad feels about this whole situation, as it is."

"Yes, I know. He's not happy about what Valerie did, but he loves Alyia and as far as he's concerned, she's my daughter." Felicia smiled at the thought of just how much her parents loved them. "'And no one, including some wet-behind-the-ears heart doctor, better try to take her from me,'" she said, mimicking her father's voice and words.

All three sisters laughed. "I swear, Dad still thinks we're five," Farrah said, her lips curled into a wide smile.

"You have to remember that even though our retired Ranger dad trained us to be equal to any man in the boardroom, on a gun range and the gym," Francine said, stopping to adjust the pillow behind her back. "We're still his baby girls, the most precious people in his life next to our mother."

"I do love it when he tells us that," Felicia admitted.

"So how's it been? Living with Griffin, I mean?" Francine asked sipping her tea.

"It hasn't been anything. I've been so busy working on this case for the past few days that I haven't seen him except for at work when we pass each other in the halls."

"How's the case going?" Francine asked.

"We're getting close."

"Let us know if you need anything. I know you're CIA, but we're family," Francine reiterated.

"I know, and thanks." Felicia said.

"What the hell does 'getting close' mean?" Farrah asked, using air quotes to express her point.

"It means she can't say more, so drop it," Francine said, chastising her sister as she tended to do because she was the oldest of the three.

Farrah folded her arms and stuck out her lip like a wounded child. Francine shot her a curt wave as she knew her next statement would perk her right back up.

"Do you need our help with anything else?" Francine asked, using a calming, mother-like voice. "Any questions you might want to ask us?"

Felicia frowned and shook her head. "I don't think so."

Farrah sighed and rolled her eyes skyward. "Girl, do you need information about…you know?"

Felicia's eyebrows flew to attention. "Seriously? I'm not sixteen and I *am* a doctor."

"Sweetheart, we know that, and I have no doubt that you understand the *mechanics* of things. I'm talking about the emotional aspect of things. What to expect before and after," Francine clarified.

"I can help you out on the mechanicals, too, if you like," Farrah added, swiveling her hips in her chair.

Felicia pressed her lips together. "No, I'm good… thanks. I'm pretty clear on my feelings for Griffin, too. Speaking of which, I think he's here. Excuse me a moment," she said, making her escape downstairs.

"Thanks for getting here so fast," Felicia greeted him. They walked up the stairs to the second floor where her sisters were waiting. "You ready for this?"

"As I'll ever be," Griffin said as they entered his family room.

"Griffin, you remember my sister Farrah," Felicia introduced.

"How could I forget?"

"You can't." Farrah smirked.

"Welcome back to the ATL," Griffin added.

"Thanks," Farrah replied.

"And this is my normal sister, Francine Montgomery." She gestured in Francine's direction.

"Hello, Griffin. I'd get up but…" she rubbed her stomach "…by the time I do—"

"No worries." Griffin took the tall, wing-backed leather chair between Francine and Farrah.

"I really appreciate you accommodating me like this. This is pretty much the last of my travel until the babies are born," she explained, patting her stomach.

"Twins, right?" His excitement was surprising.

"Yes, she's having a boy and girl," Felicia supplied, wondering if he'd actually forgotten their discussion that fast.

"That's great, congratulations," he said. "I just find multiple births fascinating."

"And congratulations to you, as well. Felicia tells me you're relishing your new role as father."

"It's been quite the learning experience, but Alyia's claimed half my heart," he said, his eyes zeroing in on Felicia's face.

Francine watched as Griffin stared at Felicia. "I'm sure she has."

The sisters spent the next hour getting to know Griffin. They found it especially fascinating that he'd grown up an only child with no access to the only other biological family he had—uncles and cousins—all because his maternal grandparents couldn't accept his father. Griffin answered questions and shared childhood stories before he was called back to the hospital.

"Thanks for that," Felicia said, walking Griffin to the door. "My sisters can be a little…"

"Protective?" he offered.

"That, too, but I was going to say unreasonable in regards to their level of acceptance of people outside our trio," Felicia said, laughing.

"I can imagine." Griffin pulled Felicia into his arms for a not-so-quick goodbye kiss.

"Now, that wasn't so difficult, was it?" Francine asked Felicia when she returned to the family room.

"Not at all," Felicia admitted.

"All right. We only have a few hours before we head back home and you back to work. Do you need any help getting ready for this weekend's ball?"

Farrah sat straighter and started clapping like an excited kid. "Yes, she does," she volunteered on Felicia's behalf.

"As a matter of fact, I could use your expertise in that area," she acknowledged.

Felicia was not looking forward to attending the ball; she was looking forward to what she hoped would happen *after* the ball. If the hot and heavy kisses they shared were any indication, Felicia was pretty sure that a mutually satisfying evening was ahead. A night she'd been waiting for and dreamed about for years with this man. Felicia was finding it hard to contain her excitement.

Chapter 24

Before Felicia knew it, several hours had passed since she'd said goodbye to her sisters and she was back at work. Felicia was in a chair at the head of the conference table, staring at all the information laid out on the whiteboard. "What am I missing?"

"There doesn't seem to be any common denominator between any of these patients," Samantha observed from her spot next to Felicia. "Except for this disease and all the treatment meds they're all on now, of course. Thankfully, that new antibiotic seems uniquely compatible with all the infected patients."

Before Felicia could respond there was a knock on the office door as it slowly opened. "Excuse me, you two," Stacy said, entering the room holding a pizza box, plates, silverware and napkins. "I thought you could use a break."

Felicia stood and slipped her feet back into her shoes. "That would be great, thanks," she said, gesturing her forward with her hand.

"No problem. I know how it is when you're trying to break down a bacterial problem," she offered.

"Care to join us?" Felicia asked.

"No, thanks. That's what you're here for, remember?" Stacy checked her watch. "I still have two meetings and an interview to conduct before I can head home. My husband is going to kill me if I miss another date night. The president will not only be looking for a deputy director, but a new executive director, as well."

"Well, you enjoy yourself," Felicia said with a laugh, opening the pizza box and taking a slice.

Samantha followed suit.

"Try not to work too late. I can't have a couple of great medical minds becoming weak and frail," she said on her way out.

Weak and frail. The words echoed in Felicia's mind as she put her focus back on the board. "Weak and frail…"

"What do you see?" Samantha asked.

Felicia gestured to the top portion of the board. "Look. What's the one thing all these folks have in common? Other than the illness and the meds they're on."

Samantha swallowed another bite and placed the pizza on a plate. "Nothing, we found no common activities."

Felicia shook her head. "Look again."

Samantha stared at the board for several moments and shrugged. "Sorry, I got nothing."

"Each of these groups could be considered *weak and frail,*" she said, using air quotes.

"Prisoners? Weak and frail? Hardly," Samantha declared.

"Their environment makes them weak." A deep crease spread across Samantha's forehead while Felicia's eyes brightened. "All these locations—" Felicia left her spot and circled all the places listed on the board "—are like a community of bacteria living, working and playing in close proximity to each other."

"Yeah, so?" Samantha said, biting into another slice of pizza.

"So…" Felicia put her left hand on her hip.

"Legionnaires' disease isn't contagious," Samantha reminded her.

"I know, but there isn't just one bacterial species inside of us. Each may relate differently to the ones surrounding it, but they all ultimately work together, except...?" Felicia prompted, raising one eyebrow.

Samantha's eyes widened with understanding. "When dangerous bacteria is *introduced* to the body."

Felicia grinned, impressed that making the connection was just as exciting for Samantha as it was for Felicia.

"So you think these people were targeted?" she asked. "That the bacteria were placed in the coolant systems on purpose to go after these *specific* people?"

"Yes," Felicia confirmed, smiling. "And all these people are responding to the same meds. It's as if a particular bacteria was created for this specific set of drugs."

"Almost as if they're some type of test subjects," Samantha added.

"Exactly like they are test subjects. We need to review the test results for each patient's blood, urine and X-rays to confirm my theory." Felicia reached for her cell phone. "I'll have the CIA send the samples they've collected from all the locations' water sources to the Grady lab so we can see if the bacteria matches. If it does, then we'll at least know the how."

"Great, but why Grady?"

"I need another setting, as well as a second set of eyes to check my research," Felicia stated, dialing her boss. "It's just one of my personal idiosyncrasies."

"I get it," Samantha said. "So once we confirm you're right, what's next?"

"Today, it's our job to find out how these folks got sick, so we can make sure it doesn't happen again." Felicia listened as her call went to voice mail. "It's up to the CIA and FBI to find the why and who, although our evidence can go a long way in helping to make that happen."

Samantha frowned. "That sucks."

Felicia laughed. "I'll think like a CIA agent for a minute and share this much with you. With the evidence we've just uncovered, the first thing I'd do is follow the money."

Samantha's face lit up. "Meaning what?"

"Meaning that I would be looking for who has profited, or would profit, from this outbreak, and *my* first stop would be to the pharmaceutical company. If it looks like a pharmacy experiment, it probably is."

Griffin walked into the brightly lit, narrow lab, an area that Felicia had been given to use at Grady Hospital, to find her wearing a red dress with her white coat and red-soled heels. She was leaning forward, looking into a microscope, one leg bent back. Felicia had on a set of earphones and Griffin stood watching as she swayed her hips, singing. He smiled, admiring Felicia's nice, round backside as he slowly approached her; she had yet to sense his presence. Griffin held the bag of food and drink he'd brought Felicia with one hand as he tapped her on the shoulder with the other.

"Griffin!" Felicia jumped, pulling the earplugs out of her ears. "You scared me."

"Sorry. I did knock before I entered. I figured you'd be stuck in this box a while tonight." His eyes landed on the number of files and vials lying in her wake. "So I thought I'd bring you dinner."

Felicia smiled and Griffin's heart skipped several beats. "That's so sweet of you. I could use a break." She led Griffin into a small kitchenette with stainless steel countertops, a refrigerator and microwave that sat off the main lab. The room had a metal table with four matching chairs.

Griffin sat the food and drink on the table. He reached

for her chair and gestured with his hand for her to take the seat. Felicia inhaled the scents and rubbed her hands together. "What's in the bag?"

Griffin took the seat across from Felicia. "Just your favorite—chicken, apple and cranberry salad with glazed pecans in a cranberry vinaigrette."

Felicia's face lit up. "It sounds wonderful, but I think I smell something more."

"Yes, you do." He reached inside the bag and pulled out a basket of homemade French fries.

"Yes!" She reached, swiped two French fries from the basket and stuffed them in her mouth.

Griffin laughed. "I know my lady." Their eyes met and Felicia gifted him with a slow, sexy smile. "When did you eat last?"

"This morning with Alyia."

"You've got to do better. Speaking of doing better, Green couldn't find you a better spot to work? This room is like a long, narrow tin can."

Felicia gave a flippant wave. "I've been in worse places." Her mind flashed back to the small shack she'd worked out of in South Korea. She'd had to put on wading boots every morning in order to walk through flooded conditions. "All I need is a cool, bright and clean place to work, and I'm fine."

"Yeah, but we have some state-of-the-art labs upstairs."

"I know, and they're all busy. This is fine," she declared, taking another bite of her food. "You headed home?"

Griffin smiled; he liked the sound of Felicia referring to his place as home, even if she didn't mean it in the way he hoped. Not yet at least. "No, I have a couple of post-op reports I'm waiting to review, so I thought I'd keep you company."

"While I appreciate the thought and the food," she said

as she bit into another French fry, "this isn't exactly the kind of work that's made for distractions."

"I understand, and I'll let you get back to it *after* you've had a break. We both know the mind needs it, even if we find it hard to take."

Felicia conceded his point and acknowledged it with a quick nod. She picked up a napkin and wiped her mouth. "Okay, fair enough. You not eating?"

"I already ate, but I was hoping you'd share some of yours. That's a pretty big basket," he said, eyeing the fries.

"I guess," Felicia said, teasingly pushing it closer to him. "How was your day?"

"Busy, but I don't want to talk about work, although you were amazing at this morning's press conference and briefing, by the way."

Felicia dropped her eyes. "Thanks. So what do you want to talk about?"

"Whatever you like," he said, taking a few fries and popping them into his mouth.

"Tell me about your parents," she said.

"There's not much to tell," Griffin replied as he wiped his mouth with a napkin.

"That can't be true," she insisted.

"Dad's from Mason, Georgia, and Mom was born in San Francisco. But when she was ten, her parents moved back to Beijing, China, where she stayed until she met and married my father."

"How did they meet?" she asked before taking another bite of her salad.

"Mom was an artist, but as you can imagine she didn't make much money at it, so she took another job as a party hostess for a friend's catering company. Dad was in town on business—"

"What kind of business? Was he doing his media thing then?"

"'His media thing,'" he repeated, laughing. "No, he was a freelance reporter at the time. He was doing a story on building a new type of military-to-military relationship between the US and China."

"Wow…"

"Dad had been embedded with the military for three months when one night he and a few of his friends went to a party where Mom was hosting and—"

"Let me guess. They met and fell in love at first sight," she proclaimed.

A wide smile spread across Griffin's face. There was a mischievous glint in his eyes. "Not exactly."

"I knew there was a story here," Felicia stated, rubbing her hands together like she was in for the scoop of a lifetime.

"Dad and his friends weren't exactly on their best behavior that night."

Felicia's eyes widened.

"See, Dad wasn't much of a drinker when he was younger, but he did have a thing for beautiful women…a lot of beautiful women."

"Like father, like son, I'm sure," she murmured. Griffin's left eyebrow rose. "Sorry, please continue."

"When Dad and his friends walked in to the party, they did what they always did, started pointing out which of the beautiful women they wanted to spend some quality time with. What he didn't count on was my mom being immune to his charms. So much so, she had him kicked out of the party."

"Seriously?"

"Yep, she told him that she was not that type of woman and to leave her the hell alone."

They both laughed. "How did he finally win her over?"

"He was a reporter. What do you think he did? He found out everything he could about her—who she was, what she liked—and he chased her. He wrote her notes, sent her fa-vorite flowers, art books—you name it—until she finally agreed to have dinner with him. She once told me that Dad had to prove he was worthy of her because she knew without a doubt that she was worthy of him."

"Some people would call what your father did stalk-ing and say that your mother was arrogant, but I say it's romantic…in a crazy kind of way," she said, laughing as she reached for her soda.

Griffin lost his train of thought when he saw Felicia's tongue reach for the straw as she wrapped her lips around it. After several sips, Felicia released the straw. "Griffin… Griffin?"

"Sorry, my mind wandered," he said, grateful his nap-kin covered his response to her.

"Everything okay?"

"Yes. Enough about my parents. Farrah and Robert—what's their deal?"

"Now, there's a story for you," she said, taking another sip of her drink.

"I bet." Griffin smirked. "How long have they been together?"

"That's hard to say," Felicia said.

"What do you mean?" His forehead crinkled.

"Well, we found out that they've been secretly mar-ried for months."

Griffin burst out laughing. "What?"

"Long story short," she said, brushing the salt off her hand. "They'd closed a case in Vegas and decided to stay and party with some of Farrah's friends. They lost a bet and ended up married. Farrah wanted out right away but Rob-ert didn't, so he tricked her into staying married to him."

"And he's still breathing?"

Felicia laughed. "She loves him. It just took her a min-ute to figure it out, but they're happy."

"What does he do?"

"Robert is head of our company's field security and he designs a number of our security systems. He and Meeks are best friends. They actually had a computer technology company that they sold for millions before they even graduated college."

"Nice. How was the rest of the visit with your sisters?"

"It was fine, but you'd swear there was a bigger age difference between us other than a mere five and ten minutes."

Griffin used another napkin to wipe his mouth. "Why… what's up?"

"They just love giving me unsolicited and unnecessary advice. Although some of it really has been great and timely."

"Like what?"

"Two years ago, Farrah convinced me and Francine to go in with her and buy an apartment building in Paris. We just recently finished the remodeling, which will come in handy with my new assignment."

"New assignment?" Griffin tilted his head slightly. By the instant crinkle in Felicia's forehead, Griffin could tell she had said more than she'd intended. "What new assignment, Felicia?"

Felicia pushed out a slow breath. "I've been offered a promotion. A combination of my current role and my boss's current job, only it's been amped up, so to speak."

"Oh…"

"Yes, additional field responsibilities have been added to the role. My boss is retiring in January and the first assignment will take me to Paris."

"For how long?" Griffin asked, his eyes narrowed.

"However long it takes to resolve the issues," she said.

"When were you planning to tell me…and what are your plans for Alyia?"

"I haven't actually accepted the role yet—"

"But you plan to accept, right?" Griffin's voice rose slightly as he leaned forward in his chair.

"Honestly, I thought I had. But now with Alyia and—"

"What…are…your plans?" he asked again, a little more forcefully than he'd intended.

Felicia sighed. "If I were to accept the position, Alyia and Ms. Ellen will travel with me, of course," she said, holding his gaze.

She's leaving you no choice. You have to tell her; you can't lose them. "You know I can't allow you to just take off with my daughter."

"She's *our* daughter," she corrected. "Although legally she's *mine* and I'm not running off anywhere. It's work and it will only be for a short time."

"You sure about that?" Griffin sat back and folded his arms, his face expressionless.

"Of course I'm sure. We'd only be out of the country a few months initially, then we'd go back and forth for a few weeks every other month," Felicia explained, confident in her assessment.

"That's not what I mean. Are you sure Alyia's legally yours?"

"What?" Felicia's forehead puckered.

Griffin had let Felicia slip through his fingers once and he wasn't prepared to let that happen again, even if that meant he had to play hardball. He was prepared to do whatever was necessary to get what he wanted: both Alyia and Felicia in his life permanently.

Griffin released a deep, slow sigh. "It seems there was a small loophole in the documents I initially signed all those years ago when I donated and stored my sperm. Whoever drafted those initial documents didn't anticipate someone wanting to do both at the same time. Due to contradictions in the language in both documents, *all* the sperm reverted back to me, which means any thing or *person* that resulted from said sperm is mine, solely, completely and legally."

Felicia's eyes widened slightly. "Wh...what?"

Griffin could see the fear in Felicia's eyes and while it was killing him to have to do it, he knew he had to make his position clear. "Alyia is legally my daughter and your position as her guardian is tenuous at best," he said, fighting to keep the emotion out of his voice.

"That can't be right," she whispered.

"It is, but feel free to have your sister check into it for you," he suggested. "You won't be taking Alyia anywhere without my permission."

"How...how long have you known this?"

"For a while, but before, it didn't matter. You are Alyia's mother in every way that counts."

"Obviously not," she murmured.

"Felicia, I can't let you cut me out of my daughter's life."

"I wouldn't do that," she said.

"Aren't you? You've already decided how things will go without even talking to me about it."

Felicia's shoulders dropped. "You're right and I'm sorry. But I'm her mother and I don't care what some lawyer told you. She is my daughter and she needs to be with me." Her voice rose slightly.

"No, she needs to be with both of us. Don't you see that?" he asked, leaning forward.

Felicia stood and wrapped her arms around her waist as though she was trying to keep herself from falling apart. He remembered how she'd do that whenever she was upset when they were in school. "I think you should go...now!"

Griffin's phone beeped before he could respond. He checked the screen and stood. "My patient's test results are in."

"Just go."

Griffin could see the unshed tears Felicia was holding

back. He wished he could kiss Felicia and reassure her that things would work out, but he really wasn't sure they could. "Let's talk tomorrow."

Felicia turned her back to him without responding. Griffin walked out of the kitchenette as Felicia was pulling out her phone. He heard her say, "I need your help."

Griffin knew then that he was in for one hell of a fight.

Chapter 25

Felicia was sitting at a table in the back of the hospital cafeteria, holding her foam cup with both hands, sipping a vanilla coffee. She had barely gotten any sleep the night before. When she wasn't pacing her room, she was staring down into Alyia's crib, trying not to wake her. Felicia watched the door and checked her watch as she waited, trying not to panic. *What if Griffin is right and I have no legal right to Alyia?* "Calm down," she murmured as she'd finally spotted the one person she hoped would ease her mind. She raised her hand and waved over the lifeline she prayed had the answers she needed.

"Well…"

"Good morning, Felicia," Fletcher Scott said, opening his arms wide for his customary embrace as he stood next to the table.

Felicia stood. "Sorry. Good morning, Fletcher," she said, stepping into his outstretched arms. "I'm just a little anxious for some good news."

"I understand," he said, taking a seat across from her.

"Coffee?" she offered.

"No, I've had my limit. Hit Starbucks before I boarded the plane, hit another when I landed. Look—" he presented his hands to her "—no shakes."

"Thank goodness for that," Felicia replied, laughing nervously. She wished she could say the same; she didn't dare present her hands.

"Good morning, Dr. Blake," three young interns called as they made their way to the breakfast burrito line.

"Good morning," Felicia replied, plastering a fake smile on her face.

"I'll get right to it. It looks like Griffin may be correct."

The light moment disappeared and Felicia's heart sank, but she kept her head up when all she wanted to do was to scream and cry. "You said *may*." Felicia knew she was reaching, but at the moment a sliver of hope was better than none at all.

"The contradictions in the documents work in Griffin's favor. The sperm belongs to him, and so do the children spawned from it—if the fetus is taken to term, that is." Fletcher looked around to make sure he wasn't overheard.

The corner of Felicia's mouth curved downward slightly. "So that's it?"

"Not exactly. There's no precedent for this—any of it. Legally and biologically, Valerie was Alyia's mother, regardless of how she became that way, and in a court of law, her wishes would hold a lot of weight…"

Felicia sensed what was coming, so she asked, "But?"

"But, technically, Valerie *did* steal Griffin's sperm," he explained. "While you could and hopefully would win in the end, Griffin could prevent you from leaving the country while this thing plays out in court, and there's no telling how long that could take. Not to mention it could get very ugly and very public."

"Public?" Her brows snapped together.

His frown matched hers. "A story like this won't stay buried once the courts get involved, no matter how hard you try. I can see the headlines now—Rich Doctors Fight Over Results of Stolen Sperm."

Felicia shook her head, picturing Griffin and his family, her sisters and maybe even a blotted-out picture of Alyia plastered all over the gossip magazines. "No, that can't happen."

"Then I suggest you two try to come up with some type of compromise."

She sank back into her seat. "I thought we were."

Fletcher leaned forward. "What happened? If you don't mind me asking?"

"My new job will take me out of the country for a few months at a time and—"

"Aw-ww," he groaned. "I thought Paris was a one-time trip. I didn't realize that much travel would still be an ongoing thing for you."

"So, you're on his side." Felicia took a drink of her coffee.

"No, I'm on Alyia's."

Felicia batted her eyes rapidly. "Alyia's?"

"She lost her mother, gained a new one along with a father, and now she could be pulled into a nasty custody battle, creating another uncertain future." Fletcher reached over and squeezed Felicia's hand. "Just because the two people who should know better can't find a way to put her needs ahead of their own."

Felicia freed her hand and wiped away a lone tear. She thought marrying a man she didn't know well enough for such a lifetime bond was more than putting Alyia's needs before her own. It was sacrificing everything she believed in about love and marriage, that they should go hand in hand so that a stable foundation meant it wasn't hitting the skids a few years after they both said "I do." She also believed that accomplishing everything she set out to do on a professional level was equally important, and that a woman could have it all—especially if she had the kind of support system in place that she knew existed.

"My job..." She couldn't get the words past the lump in her throat.

"I know how important your career is to you," Fletcher acknowledged. "You've worked very hard and sacrificed a lot to get where you are, and it's not like you asked for any of this."

"And neither did Alyia. I love my daughter and she has to be the priority."

Fletcher smiled. "Why didn't you let Farrah look into this for you? It's right up her alley."

Felicia laughed. "Really, do you even need to ask?"

"Good point," he said, scratching his head. "Farrah would most definitely attack Griffin with guns, arrows and knives blazing...literally."

"Exactly."

"Excuse me, Dr. Blake, but you asked that I come find you when the next set of genetic samples are ready for your review," a male nurse said, his eyes darting between Felicia and Fletcher, lingering a little longer on her guest than mere curiosity warranted.

"Thanks, Luther, I'll be right up."

The nurse nodded and rushed away, but not before a final look at Fletcher.

"Looks like you're making yourself at home here at Grady Memorial."

Felicia stood and Fletcher followed suit. "This is only a temporary stop," she said. "I'll be back in Texas before you know it."

"I hope to change her mind about that," a familiar voice said, coming to stand next to Felicia. "Dr. Griffin Kaile," he said to Fletcher, offering his hand.

"Fletcher Scott. Pleased to meet you." Fletcher accepted his hand, giving it a firm shake, though Griffin appeared to be sizing the other man up.

"Fletcher is an old family friend," Felicia supplied reluctantly. She didn't want to show her hand too much should she find herself in some kind of custody fight.

"Well, I really need to get going." Fletcher hugged Felicia. "Take care of yourself and reach out if you need anything." He looked over his shoulder and said, "Dr. Kaile."

Griffin answered with a stoic, "Fletcher Scott."

Griffin and Felicia watched Fletcher thread his way through the crowd, ignoring the inquisitive looks from the women he passed as he made it to the glass doors and left.

"You got a second?" Griffin asked.

Felicia checked her watch. "Actually, I don't," she said through a fake smile. She didn't want to bring on any more attention from the curious patrons having breakfast.

"Please, Felicia," he pleaded, reaching for her hand. "I heard you pacing most of the night. I didn't get much sleep, either, and you left so early this morning. I don't want another night like last night."

Felicia sighed deeply. "Neither do I," she admitted, holding his gaze.

"Please sit, it'll only take a moment," Griffin reassured her.

"Okay."

"I want to apologize for coming across so strong last night," he said. "I wasn't trying to hurt you. I just…"

Felicia bit her bottom lip. "I understand." She knew Griffin was just as scared of losing Alyia as she was.

"Do you? Do you really?" Griffin challenged.

"Yes, and I think we can figure this thing out," she said, nodding slowly. "Just as long as we both remember to put Alyia's needs ahead of our own. And you were right, she needs us both."

"All right, then. How about we both agree not to make any major decisions about anything until after this weekend? Let's just get through the ball and your case, and then we can sit down and go over all of our options."

Felicia gave him a half smile. "Sounds like a plan." Then her gaze narrowed on him. "Now, how did you know I was close to wrapping up my case?"

"I saw Dr. Gray a little bit ago and she mentioned it to me."

"Did she, now?" she asked, frowning.

"I am a department head. She was briefing us on the latest turn of events. She seems very impressed with you… and especially your work."

"Speaking of which, I guess I should get to it." Felicia stood.

"Me, too." Griffin rose and planted a not-so-quick kiss on Felicia's lips. "Damn, I needed that. By the way, who was that Fletcher guy?"

Felicia threw her head back, brought her hand to her heart and laughed. Something she hadn't thought she'd be able to do anytime soon twenty-four hours ago. "You just can't help yourself. Fletcher really is an old family friend that works for my family from time to time. His visit was strictly business. That's it."

A big smile crawled across his face. "I'll see you later, baby."

"Baby?" she whispered after him. A man who could apologize and compromise was a man worth keeping around.

Griffin sighed before cutting the engine to his Porsche. After spending the night thinking he'd done irreparable damage to his relationship with Felicia, hurting the woman he loved…the mother of his child, Griffin was determined to find a way to make things right. He was going to do what was best for both Felicia and Alyia, no matter what it cost him personally. But first he had to tell his parents about them both.

"Here goes nothing," he said as he exited the vehicle.

Walking up to the door of his childhood home always brought back fond memories. He hoped that the news he was about to share with his parents would be the beginning of many more memories for his family. Griffin lifted his knuckled fist to wrap it against the mahogany carved door but the left side of the grand double entrance opened.

"Good evening, Master Griffin," their longtime butler greeted him, wearing his customary uniform: black suit, white shirt and black tie.

"Good evening, Jasper. I thought we talked about that 'master' stuff."

"You talked, I ignored," he quipped, stepping aside so Griffin could enter the Colonial mansion where he grew up.

Griffin laughed. "My parents around?"

"Of course," he replied, frowning at Griffin as though he'd just asked the most ridiculous question. "It's tea time."

Griffin smirked at the disappointed expression on Jasper's face. "Of course, what was I thinking?"

The Kaile mansion was a magnificent display of opulence and wealth. The mixture of traditional Asian and American furnishings spoke to Griffin's blended lineage perfectly. Marble floors and a row of tall vases led the way to the sitting area. The doors opened onto a beautifully decorated room with Oriental rugs, cathedral windows and a leather sofa and chairs.

Griffin walked into the sitting room to find his parents across from each other in matching green leather wing-backed chairs, a small glass table between them holding a cherry-blossom Chinese teapot and two matching handle-less cups. The poetic motif of pastel blue flowers matched the framed tapestry that hung over the stone fireplace.

"Griffin, darling, what a nice surprise," his mother said, placing her cup down on the table. She opened her arms and, as expected, Griffin bent to hug his mother.

"This is a nice surprise, son," his father said, holding

out his hand, which Griffin quickly accepted and shook. "Care to join us?"

"Shall I bring in another cup?" Jasper asked from his spot at the threshold.

"When have you ever seen me join my parents for tea, Jasper?"

"One can always hope," Jasper said with a note of sarcasm before turning to leave.

Griffin faced his parents, whose expectant faces said they were concerned. "I hate to disturb you, but I need to speak to you both about something very important."

Lin Kaile's eyes narrowed slightly as she picked up her cup again. "I'm not going to like this, am I?" she declared, sipping her tea.

"Let the boy speak, dear."

Griffin shoved his hands into the pockets of the leather jacket he wore as he gave his parents the CliffsNotes version of how he'd suddenly found himself with a daughter and Felicia as her mother. The silence was expected, but he was shocked when it was his father who recovered first.

"So, you decided to store your sperm so you would have a legacy in the event something ever happened to you," his father asked, the words both direct and unemotional, coming from a man he respected more than anyone.

Griffin wasn't sure if his father was asking him a question, but he figured he'd better not take any chances so he said, "Yes, sir."

"And you donated sperm to further stem cell research?"

"Yes, sir," Griffin replied.

"Hmm…"

"Hmm? Is that all you have to say to your idiotic son?" Lin snapped, her brows knitting together. "Grif…say something!"

His mother meant business whenever that private nickname for her husband was used, and definitely if her voice had reached that raised tone.

"I'm proud of you, son," he finally said.

"What?" she said, getting to her feet so fast she nearly spilled her tea.

"You wanted me to speak, so let me speak, my love," his father said in Mandarin, removing the shaking cup and saucer from her hand and placing it on the table. He rarely spoke in his wife's native language, but when he did it always touched her heart.

Lin sighed and replied in English, "Yes, love."

They shared a smile before returning their attention to their son. "Sit down," his father said.

Griffin pulled up a chair and took the empty space on the left side of the table near his father. "I'm very proud of you because your heart was in the right place. However, if you wanted to do something so drastic, you should have talked to us. We could have helped you ensure your privacy as well as your security."

"Yes, sir," Griffin said, duly chastised.

"Now, tell us about our granddaughter."

A smile spread across Griffin face. "She's perfect... beautiful. Here's her picture." Griffin took out his phone and pulled up several images for them to view.

Lin sat forward and her husband got up and went to stand next to her chair so they could view the pictures together.

"Oh, my," Lin said, offering the most genuine smile he'd seen since before he'd refused to propose to Jia. "She has your eyes, Griffin."

"I know," he replied proudly.

"And your cheekbones," Griffin's father said, sliding the back of his hand down his wife's face.

Lin giggled and Griffin smiled.

The exchange was like so many he'd witnessed over the

years. He'd never thought passionate love could be maintained over the years, but to see them now from a different perspective, thanks to Felicia, Griffin had to rethink that position.

Lin smiled. "So Felicia is Alyia's guardian," she confirmed.

Griffin pushed his shoulders back and sat straight. "Felicia is Alyia's mother," he clarified. "And I'm going to do everything in my power to make us a family. It's the right thing and it's what's best for Alyia."

"I can see that," his father said.

Lin lifted an eyebrow. "I believe you think it's best for you, too."

Griffin stood and walked away from his parents, over to the fireplace. He exhaled. "I do. She makes me…"

"Weak," his parents said in unison.

Griffin smiled.

"Well, that's that," Griffin's father said to his wife, taking her hand in his. "Let's go, honey. Time to meet our granddaughter."

Chapter 26

Felicia stood in front of the long mirror and smirked. For the first time in a long while, she actually enjoyed the sight before her. Felicia still wasn't used to having her shoulders and the tops of her breasts so prominently displayed, but had to admit that the black, strapless, silhouette Valentino gown with cascading side panels screamed sexy, understated elegance. The black Christian Louboutin shoes, diamond choker and matching earrings and bracelet were the perfect complement.

"My…my, you look gorgeous. I love that half-up, half-down hairstyle thing you did, too," Ms. Ellen complimented her from the threshold of Felicia's bedroom.

"Thank you," she said to Ms. Ellen's reflection.

"Griffin won't know what to do with himself when he sees you." She offered a teasing smile.

"That's the idea," she whispered, turning to face Ms. Ellen. Felicia couldn't help but shiver at the thought that Griffin just might have a few ideas. Especially since that intimate exchange a few days ago had ended so abruptly.

"Tonight's pretty important to Griffin, his family and that fancy foundation of theirs, but you remember something, young lady," Ms. Ellen said, pointing her index finger at Felicia.

"What's that?"

"You and that baby sleeping down the hall are pretty important to him, too."

Felicia beamed. "I know."

"Well, you better go." She swatted playfully after her. "He's downstairs waiting for you."

"Don't hesitate to call if you need us." Felicia scooped her clutch from off the bed.

"I won't need to, nor will I call," she said with a reassuring pat on her shoulder. "Just go enjoy each other. I have everything covered here. As always."

Felicia gave Ms. Ellen a hug and walked out of the room. She stopped at the top of the stairs and stared down at the Greek god–like figure wearing a perfectly cut Italian tuxedo. Griffin was facing the door, putting something in his pocket, and only turned at the sound of Felicia's stiletto-covered feet hitting the first marble step.

Griffin felt as though his heart had actually stopped for a moment. "My God, you're magnificent," he said, his mouth slightly open.

Felicia descended the steps slowly, keeping her eyes on Griffin and her hand on the rail. When she hit the final ones, Griffin reached for her hand and helped her the rest of the way down. "Thank you. You look pretty terrific yourself."

"Thanks," he said, bringing her hand to his lips for a kiss. "Ready?" Griffin offered his arm.

"As I'm ever going to be." Felicia wrapped her arm around his. "After the prep necessary to look like this, I hope I can stay awake," she replied, offering up a small smile.

Griffin stopped and turned to face her. "I'm incredibly proud of you. To figure out that all the Legionnaires' cases came from the same bacterial source generated in the pharmaceutical lab that was trying to get a key ingredient for a specific cocktail of meds expedited was brilliant."

"I got to work with a wonderful group of people at the CDC, and my CIA team is always on point. They're very good at their jobs. They followed the money and I followed the science. Finding the white-collar bad guys was easy. Chasing down the local bad guys is a little more challenging."

"I'm sure they'll gather them all up. Enough of that. Let's go enjoy our evening. I promise it will be a night we both remember." Griffin intended to give Felicia a sweet and gentle kiss, only his desire for her got the best of him for a moment. He took her mouth as if this was the last chance he'd ever have to kiss her so he needed to make the most of it. When Griffin finally let Felicia up for air, he whispered, "That should hold me until later."

Griffin stared at Felicia, enjoying the rise and fall of her breast. "I can't wait," Felicia whispered.

After a relatively short limo ride, Griffin was escorting a smiling Felicia into the grand ballroom of the Ritz-Carlton Hotel. The space was immaculately decorated in a winter wonderland theme. From the white-and-silver wall coverings, the whitewashed wooden dance floor and the gorgeous crystal chandeliers, to each table set with a silver-and-white mini Christmas tree centerpiece with Hershey's candy kisses dropping from its leaves.

"Oh, my..."

"Yes, Mother tends to go all out for this every year."

"Everything is beautiful...so elegantly placed, right down to the white-and-silver place settings and crystal glasses."

"That's Mother," he confirmed. "Everything must be perfect."

"She certainly doesn't think I'm perfect," she teased. "Not for you, anyway."

Griffin gave Felicia's hand a gentle squeeze. "You'd be surprised. Anyway, I think you're perfect for me and that's all that matters."

"If you say so," she replied.

Griffin could see he still had some convincing to do and he intended to do just that. Well, as soon as they'd spent an appropriate amount of time at the event.

"Darling, there you are," Lin called out as she approached. The black-and-white, tea-length gown she wore shimmered with every move.

Griffin kissed her on both cheeks. "Mother."

"Mrs. Kaile, you look beautiful, and these decorations are gorgeous," Felicia said by way of compliments.

"Thank you. We do have a particular image we want to uphold," she said, glancing around the room as though trying to take everything in from a newcomer's point of view. "You look quite lovely yourself." Lin gifted her with a big smile.

"Thank you," she finally said.

Lin turned her back to Felicia. "Griffin, both the mayor and the lieutenant governor are here and asking for you."

"I see them," he replied, spotting the area where the two men were holding court with his father and several of the hospital board members, who were probably hitting them up for additional donations. "Shall we?" He reached for Felicia's hand.

"No, you go ahead," she urged. "I've had my political fill for the day."

"I'm sure you have." Griffin gave Felicia a quick kiss on the cheek. "Mother, I hope you caught the news conference regarding the wonderful work Felicia and her team did solving the country's recent medical mystery."

Lin acknowledged her son with a slow-building wide smile before turning to face Felicia. "I most certainly did. I have no doubt about what a capable doctor and medical investigator you are," she said, offering Felicia quick nod of her head.

Griffin kissed Felicia on the cheek again before saying, "I'll be right back."

Felicia nodded and accepted a glass of champagne from a passing waiter. She wasn't sure she'd heard Lin correctly when she'd complimented her on her work at first until she noticed that her smile had actually reached her eyes and she'd offered her a respectful nod.

"I really do commend your work ethic," Lin repeated, accepting a small plate of hors d'oeuvres that was being passed around.

"But not much else, right?" Felicia replied, looking at the obstinate woman over the rim of her champagne glass, swaying to the up-tempo song the band was playing.

Lin tilted her head slightly. "You don't think that I believe you're good enough for my son." She bit into a shrimp-and-cheese combination. Felicia remained silent, hoping that would be enough of an answer for her. "Well, you're right. He's my son, and I don't think anyone is."

"Except Jia."

Lin scoffed. "Jia knew what she wanted and was prepared to do whatever she felt was necessary to get it."

"Like give up her life." The words flew out of Felicia's mouth before she could stop them.

Lin smirked. "Oh, my dear, Jia doesn't *have* a life, other than the desire to be someone's wife and mother. I'm not saying that's a bad thing, it's just not the only thing."

Felicia frowned. "I don't understand."

Lin sighed, as though having to explain her words to a child. "As Alyia grows, you'll feel the same way. No one will be good enough, no matter how wrong you may be."

Felicia's eyes widened. "Excuse me?"

Lin waved and smiled at everyone that passed, and for

some reason they all seemed to know better than to interrupt. "My son's feelings for you make him weak. Just as my and my husband's feelings for each other make us weak."

"Is that a bad thing?" Felicia murmured, staring down into her glass.

"Not at all, when it's reciprocated. You see, my dear, my husband and I fought wars to be together and I believe my son would go to war with, and for, you, if that's what it took to have you. Actually, both you and Alyia."

"Again—"

Lin brought her half-curled index finger to her lips. "What I'm not sure about is…are you willing to fight just as hard for him?" She let that settle a moment before adding, "Anything less would be unacceptable for him…as it should be for you. Being a wife and a mother doesn't have to be the only thing. While in my opinion it should be the main one, it just *can't* be the last thing."

Felicia brought her glass to her lips, slowly sipping the bubbly concoction while absorbing the woman's words, weighing them against the choices she would soon have to make in her own life.

"I see my determined son headed your way, so if you'll excuse me," Lin said before sweeping away, leaving a hint of jasmine scent behind along with much for Felicia to ponder.

Griffin approached, removed the glass from Felicia's hand and placed it on the nearby table. He led her out onto the dance floor filled with Atlanta's movers and shakers as he maneuvered his way to the center, where he pulled Felicia into his arms. "They're playing our song," he whispered in her ear.

Felicia leaned her head back, looked into Griffin's eyes and asked, "We have a song?"

"We do now." His hand snaked around Felicia's waist as her hands climbed his chest, coming to rest around his neck. Soon their bodies moved slowly to the band's rendition of The O'Jays' "Forever Mine."

Griffin's growing response to their movements made its presence known. Felicia's body was reacting in an all-too-familiar manner that he easily provoked. When the music came to an end, Griffin looked into Felicia's eyes, resting his right hand on the side of her face. "Let's get out of here, baby," he said, his voice husky.

She was too aroused to respond with anything more than a nod.

Griffin intertwined their hands and walked off the dance floor, but before they could make their escape, their path was blocked by a determined-looking Dr. Trent Green.

Trent held out his hand toward Felicia. "May I have this next dance?"

Felicia could feel Griffin stiffen at her side; she squeezed his hand, but kept her eyes on Trent. "We were actually about to leave. Maybe next time."

"Of course," Trent said, dropping his hand.

"Good evening, Dr. Green," Griffin said with a small smirk before heading in the direction of the exit.

Felicia glanced around the room as they made their escape, spotting Lin Kaile, who raised her glass and offered her a small nod. Felicia accepted the encouraging gesture with a smile.

Griffin led Felicia through the lobby and out to the waiting limousine. "Thanks for not going all caveman on me," Felicia said, smiling up at Griffin as they stood next to the car.

"It wasn't easy. The idea of you in any man's arms other than mine is hard to handle."

Felicia cupped Griffin's face in her hands. "You don't have that to worry about."

Griffin covered Felicia's hand with his, brought it to his

lips and kissed her palm. "I know, baby. Tonight you're all mine."

Felicia shivered at the thought. Betty Wright's "Tonight Is the Night" popped into her head. Unlike the woman in the song, Felicia wasn't nervous and all her tremors were related to her desire for Griffin. While she had no idea what lay ahead for her, she couldn't wait to find out.

Chapter 27

Griffin helped Felicia into the limousine but remained outside the vehicle. "Everything all set?" he asked his driver.

"Yes, sir."

"Great, give me five minutes and take off," he instructed.

Griffin slid in next to Felicia in the limousine and captured her hand between his. "Do you trust me?"

"Yes," she whispered.

"I got us a room for the night at a hotel down the street. Ms. Ellen is aware of where we'll be if she needs us. But if you're not ready…"

Felicia leaned forward and kissed him gently on the lips. "I'm ready."

Griffin buried his hands in Felicia's curls as he devoured her lips, moaning into her mouth. Felicia pulled at Griffin's shoulders like she couldn't get close enough to him, and the movement had Griffin fighting for control. He had to be gentle and wanted the night to be special; Felicia deserved that. The thought of being the only man to ever have her made completing that task even harder. Griffin battled his desire to take her in the back of the car and forced himself to stop when he felt it pull away from the curb.

After a few short minutes they walked into the presidential suite of the Glenn Hotel. Griffin studied her face and movements, watching for any signs of hesitation on Felicia's part.

"Wow, this is gorgeous." Felicia entered and placed her purse on the bar as she admired the beautifully decorated room. The cream-and-gray high-backed sofa and matching chairs in front of the wood-burning fireplace were a romantic complement to the cathedral windows allowing in the lights of the city to flow in.

Felicia picked up a bottle of wine lying on a bed of ice in a silver bucket on the glass table. "Very nice."

"I hope so," he said, walking up behind her. "Shall I pour?"

Felicia pushed out a breath and turned to face Griffin. "Later." Felicia took a step back. "Mind if I get comfortable?"

"Of course not. The bedroom is over there," Griffin turned slightly to his left and pointed to a closed door. When he turned back, he found that Felicia hadn't moved and was staring up at him with glassy eyes. "Are you okay, baby?"

Felicia felt eerily calm in spite of her pounding heart. She offered Griffin a half smile and said, "Yes, I'm fine, but I don't want wine clouding this moment. And I don't want to be in a room away from you when I do this…"

She removed her earrings and bracelet, dropping them on the table. Felicia reached to the side of her dress and slowly lowered the hidden zipper. The wider Griffin's eyes became, the bolder she felt. "You see, I've never done anything like this before and I want to experience every minute of it." Felicia's dress fell to the floor and she stood in a La Perla strapless, white-lace bra and panty set.

Griffin sucked in an audible breath and Felicia bit her lip as she wrapped her index finger around the string on her right hip.

"Don't," Griffin whispered, his voice cracking. "Before we go any further, I want you to know that I'm in love with you. I think I have been since that first day you ran into Dr. Jacobson's class."

Emotions she couldn't name engulfed her and a lone tear slid down Felicia's face. "I think that's when I fell in love with you, too."

A slow, sexy smile spread across Griffin's face and Felicia trembled. He walked up and circled Felicia, coming to stand behind her. Griffin swept her hair to the side, removed her choker necklace and placed it next to her other jewelry before kissing her behind the ear. He slid his tongue down her neck to her shoulder, where he kissed her again. Griffin placed his hands over hers and held them at her hips. "Please, let me take it from here."

Felicia leaned back into Griffin, raising her arms and wrapping her hands around his neck. "Whatever you want, baby."

Griffin used his left hand to caress Felicia's breasts while sliding his right hand slowly down her stomach and under her panties. His fingers slid through the damp curls covering her sex several times before slipping first one, then another, inside her.

"Oh, yes...yes." Felicia's hips met each slow, deliberate thrust of his hand as she moaned his name.

"Let go, baby...just let go. For me...only me," he whispered, increasing his strokes.

"Griffin...oh, Griffin." Felicia's voice mounted from a harsh whisper to a full-blown, high-pitched scream.

Felicia's knees buckled and Griffin swept her off her feet and out of her heels. He carried her to the bedroom, placed her in the center of the bed and removed her bra. Griffin quickly divested himself of his own clothes, removing condom packets from his pocket and tossing them on the bed.

Griffin hovered over Felicia like a helicopter. He used his tongue and lips to explore Felicia's body from navel to breasts, where he paid extra-special attention. He sucked and teased her nipples while his fingers played between her legs, sending her over the edge before he even removed her panties. As Felicia lay gasping for breath, he rolled on the thin veil of protection before sliding down her body. Griffin used both hands to raise her hips as if he was about to enjoy his favorite meal. He untied the ties of her panties with his teeth and slowly removed her essence-soaked cloth, allowing the aroma of arousal to fill the room.

"I'm crazy about you, Felicia." Griffin kissed her virgin lips, using his tongue to reintroduce himself to her sex. While every male instinct demanded that he claim what was now his, Griffin knew he had to make sure Felicia's body was ready for the invasion he'd soon unleash. He teased with his fingers and tongue, the taste of her like the sweetest of fruit.

"Please, Griffin…show me…baby, please…"

Griffin rose and stared into Felicia's eyes as he held himself at her entrance. "I love you."

"I love you…"

Griffin slowly pushed into Felicia, stopping long enough for her body to adjust to his size and girth. "Don't stop… please, baby. Don't hold back," Felicia cried, wrapping her legs around his waist.

He kissed her as he thrust forward, pushing through

that silken barrier. Felicia sucked in a quick breath and Griffin stopped. "Are you okay, baby?"

"Oh, yes…yes," she sighed, raising her hips to meet his downward thrust.

Before long they'd found a comfortable rhythm that made stopping nearly impossible. Felicia had never felt so fulfilled before and she knew she'd never get tired of that feeling. Too soon, her body tensed and claimed its release, causing Griffin to race forward toward his own final satisfaction.

As they both lay quiet on the bed, Felicia's mind raced. After everything they'd just done, Felicia still wanted him. How could she have ever thought she could stay away from this man? She ran her hand through the fine, sweat-soaked hairs on Griffin's chest and smiled. She lowered her hand and grabbed his shaft and began to caress it, paying special attention to its tip. Within moments Griffin sighed and his eyes slowly opened.

"Don't poke the animal unless you want to get poked back."

Felicia laughed, looking up into his eyes as she continued to stroke him. "That's the idea, baby."

"It's too soon, my love. Your body needs to recover. I didn't hold back that much," he told her, stroking her face with his right hand.

Felicia may have been a virgin, but there was one thing she was pretty sure she could do and couldn't wait to try. Felicia giggled. "I wasn't talking about me," she said before sliding down Griffin's body and taking him into her mouth.

She sucked, pulled and teased Griffin with her tongue, enjoying every moment of it. It was as if she'd just discovered a new treat she was determined to savor.

"Damn, baby…so…good." Soon he tried to free himself. "I'm going…to…oh…baby."

Griffin's words only seemed to motivate Felicia more. She continued to pull and suck until Griffin finally exploded. Felicia felt a powerful level of satisfaction that she never knew was possible.

Griffin pulled Felicia up into his arms. "Please tell me you've never done *that* before," he panted between breaths.

Felicia burst out laughing. "Absolutely not."

Griffin kissed Felicia and held her until they both drifted off into a peaceful sleep.

The next morning Felicia woke to her name being whispered and the smells of vanilla and honey rolling off Griffin's body. Since his hair was wet, Felicia assumed he'd already had his shower. Griffin leaned across the bed and whispered, "Good morning, baby." His voice sent waves of desire throughout Felicia's body; her nipples responded instantly.

Felicia used the sheet to cover her mouth. "Good morning," she murmured through the sheet, fearing a bad case of morning breath.

Griffin pulled the sheets down and kissed her forehead. "That's better," he said, smiling.

Felicia sighed.

"You have twenty minutes to bathe before breakfast arrives," Griffin ordered.

Felicia sat up in bed, her long, curly hair falling forward, covering her breasts. "What?"

Griffin scanned her face before his eyes zeroed in on her breasts. "Damn, you're beautiful. Sweetheart, you need to soak."

Felicia moved her legs and realized why he'd say such a thing. She bit down on her lip. After everything they'd done last night, how could she be embarrassed? "That's your fault," she reminded him.

"Damn right," he proudly declared. "I talked to Ms. Ellen and Alyia's fine. I told her we would see them sometime this afternoon. *Late* afternoon."

"Did you, now? So what do you have in mind?" she asked, giving him a sexy smile.

"You'll see. But first, you bathe and then we eat."

Griffin left Felicia alone and she made her way to the bathroom, her muscles protesting with each step. She reached for the toothbrush and realized it was hers. In fact, all the toiletries that lay in front of her were hers. Just as the realization set in of what Griffin must have done, he knocked on the door.

"Yes," she sang.

"I thought you'd like a little java while you soak." Griffin handed her a cup of coffee.

She accepted it with a big smile as she took a sip and said, "Chocolate mocha with whipped cream… My things… And I assume there are clothes somewhere here, too? You really thought of everything."

"I tried to, and I had a little help," he admitted.

"Ms. Ellen?" Felicia used her tongue to swipe a dollop of whipped cream.

"Yes. We can't have you leaving this hotel in your party dress as though you were making the walk of shame. There is no shame here." Griffin kissed her on the temple. "Now, enjoy your bath. When you're done, put on the robe that's on the bed and meet me in the living room."

Felicia noticed he was wearing the same robe and smiled as a warm feeling of anticipation spread through her body. She followed instructions, allowing her muscles to recover and prepare for what she knew would be another robust round of lovemaking. She couldn't wait. Though, they still had one pretty big hurdle to jump before they could find any semblance of happily-ever-after. The conversations with Lin and her own mother featured prominently in her thoughts as she also thought about her recent conversation with Dr. Stacy Gray and her boss Steven. Felicia sighed. "You know what you have to do."

She stepped out of the tub, wrapped her hair in a towel and dried off. She went to the bedroom and found the large white robe lying on the bed. She enveloped her body in the robe, placed her cup on the dresser and reached for her phone. Felicia dialed the number that had been captured in her memory and within seconds her call was answered. "Good morning, it's Felicia. I'm in."

"You sure? What about—?"

"You let me worry about that," she said before ending the call.

Felicia tightened her robe, picked up her coffee cup and went to find Griffin.

Griffin was surveying the few office buildings in the city coming to life on a Sunday morning while drinking his coffee when he heard the bedroom door open. He turned to see a robe-clad, barefoot Felicia holding her coffee cup and heading for him. Griffin's body immediately came to life. "You are so amazing and you're finally mine," he whispered in Mandarin.

"Did you mean to say all that out loud?" she replied in English, her lips curved in a sexy smile.

"Probably not," he said, pulling Felicia into his arms, kissing her passionately on the lips.

"Where's breakfast?" Felicia asked when Griffin finally let her up for air.

"It should be here in about thirty minutes. I waited to place the order. I didn't want it to get cold." Griffin released Felicia's hair from the towel.

"What are you doing?" she asked.

Griffin gifted her with a childlike smile. "I love your hair when it's wet and curly."

Felicia rolled her eyes and smiled.

"How do you feel?" he asked, staring down into her eyes, wrapping a few strands around his fingers.

"Wonderful." Felicia's smile widened as she pulled at his robe's tie. "Have any idea about what we can do while we wait for the food to arrive?"

"Several, but we really should talk."

"Spoilsport. Is there more coffee?" she asked.

"Yes, let me," he offered, refilling her cup, adding two teaspoons of cream before handing it back to her. Griffin guided Felicia to the sofa.

"Thank you," she said, taking a seat.

"About—"

"Look—"

They both laughed. "You go first," Felicia offered, sipping her coffee.

"I know how important your work is to you and I wouldn't want you to not have the career you've worked so hard for, even if that means you're chasing dangerous viruses across the world." Griffin pressed his lips together for a moment. "But I can't have you dragging our daughter after you."

"I won't—"

"Let me finish." He covered her lips with his hands. "I love you and I want us to be a family, so go when and where you have to. Alyia and I will be here waiting for you to get back. And if you're somewhere safe for Alyia, we'll come visit you, no matter what I have to drop here in order to make that happen."

Felicia sighed and smiled. "You'd do that…for me?"

"I'll do that for us."

Felicia kissed him. "That won't be necessary."

"What?" Griffin frowned.

"I resigned from the CIA," she said in a nonchalant manner, sipping her coffee.

"What...when?"

Felicia's eyes darted skyward briefly. "Umm, yester-day."

"Why?" His frown deepened.

"Let's just say a friend reminded me that I'm a mom now. My life is no longer my own. I have a daughter and a family to think about," she said, holding his gaze. She put her mug down on the table and cupped her hands in her lap.

"I can't pretend that I'm not happy to hear that you won't be traipsing around the world all the time, but what will you do?" Griffin ran the back of his hand down the side of her face. "You're too talented a doctor not to share your gift. Do you have any idea what you're going to do now?"

"As a matter of fact, I do." Felicia offered him a cheeky smile. "I've accepted a position at the CDC right here in Atlanta. I'm going to be working for Stacy Gray."

Griffin's eyebrows stood at attention. "What...when did that happen?"

"About ten minutes ago."

"There's only one position that I'm aware of that some-one of your caliber should be interested in and that's the Deputy Director of the CDC."

"That would be the position." She winked.

"Well, damn."

Feeling happier and bolder than ever, Felicia folded her arms across her chest. "So, is the whole marriage idea still on the table?"

Griffin threw his head back and laughed. He unfolded her arms and intertwined their hands. "My parents got married on their own. My Chinese grandparents couldn't accept my mother marrying a black man. My parents were young and broke, so my dad used a Cracker Jack box ring when he married my mother. He promised to buy her the perfect ring one day and he'd re-propose. It took seven times and seven different rings before he got it right."

Felicia smiled. "I can imagine what that ring looks like."

"You don't have to." Griffin kissed her on the corner of her lips.

"What?"

"Check your pocket," he said as he stared into her eyes.

Felicia quickly pulled her hands free and felt inside both pockets. A shaking right hand came out with a small black pouch.

Griffin smiled and took it from her hand. "Let me."

He opened it, took Felicia's hand and dropped a two-carat, princess-cut diamond, ruby and emerald ring into her palm. It was simple, beautiful and completely unexpected.

"Griffin, it's outstanding."

Griffin took the ring and held it between his thumb and index finger. "My mother said it had always been just her and Dad, even after having me. They have an unbreakable bond, which is what the diamond represents. Mother said they stood strong together through the good and the bad times, which is what the ruby and emeralds stand for. Mother wanted a ring that reflected their story. So no matter how much money my dad made or how big the diamonds he offered her, it took this final ring—" he shook it a couple of times "—a symbol of what they'd always been…for him to get it right."

"Now she's given it to you?" Felicia asked, her voice barely above a whisper.

"No, she's given it to *us*."

"Us…"

"Mother always knew you were The One. She just wanted to make sure *you* knew it. Nothing makes people realize how important they are to each other like a little adversity from those that matter most." Griffin wiped away tears Felicia didn't realized she had shed.

"You know they say women find love too soon and men

find it too late?" Felicia held out her left hand. "I think *we* found it right on time."

Griffin slid the ring onto Felicia's finger. "I think you're right, baby," Griffin agreed before kissing her passionately on the lips.

Epilogue

"**O**nly Francine could actually have her babies on their due date," Felicia said, laughing as she paced the maternity waiting area of the Texas Women's Hospital. The brightly lit room with its expensive, low-backed leather seating had televisions on three walls and was very cozy.

"Talk about bad timing." Farrah's eyes zeroed in on her husband, who was standing across the room talking to Griffin, who was holding his and Felicia's daughter. "Valentine's Day, of all days."

"I'm sure whatever crazy thing you two have planned will keep," Felicia replied, giving her sister the side-eye.

Farrah smirked. "It most certainly will. Now sit down. You're making me dizzy."

Felicia rolled her eyes and complied, taking a seat across from her sister. "I think it'll be cool to have Valentine's Day babies."

"Of course you do. You did get married on New Year's Eve," Farrah reminded.

Felicia's eyes found her husband and smiled. "Yes, I did."

"Newlywed love, isn't it divine?" Farrah teased.

"Yes, it is. Speaking of divine love, have you heard from Mom and Dad yet?" Felicia asked.

"Yes, the weather in Colorado is still pretty bad. All the snow they're getting is great for skiing but not so much for flying."

"I know Mom is going nuts." Felicia shook her head.

Farrah looked over at Robert, who was now reaching for a laughing Alyia. "She was, until my brilliant husband was able to work with the resort's technology team to set up a system so Mom and Dad can watch the birth of their second and third grandchildren." Both Felicia and Farrah trained their eyes on Alyia, who was bending her body from side to side, playing a peekaboo game with her father from her uncle's arms. "Hopefully they'll be here tomorrow."

"Robert's going to make a great dad someday," Felicia predicted.

Farrah's mouth curved into a smile and her eyes sparkled like she had a secret she couldn't wait to spill. "Well, Griffin certainly has taken to fatherhood."

"Yes, he has." Felicia smiled, biting down on her lip.

"So, things good at work? Are you and your boss still getting along?" Farrah crossed her legs.

"Yeah, Stacy's great. Why are you asking?" Felicia frowned.

"I was just making sure you were still happy with your decision to leave the CIA. I'm so happy you're a quick plane ride away versus being on the other side of the world." Farrah pulled Felicia into a quick embrace.

"Someone's emotional today," Felicia teased.

"Shut up," Farrah said, giving her sister a playful shove.

"Excuse me," an older nurse called as she entered the waiting room. "If you all would please follow me."

Griffin reached for Felicia's hand as he held Alyia in his other arm and Robert wrapped his arm around Farrah's waist, and they all followed the nurse.

"Knock…knock," the nurse called as she opened the

door to a hospital suite that seemed to be designed for royalty. "I have some people excited to meet their new family members."

Everyone entered the bright room filled with natural light offered by the extra-large corner window. The room had dark hardwood flooring, a queen-size poster bed placed in the middle of the circular room and designer furnishings. Francine, sitting up against the headboard, her hair up in a large bun, was wearing a white silk robe. She hardly looked like a woman who had just gone through several hours of labor. In her arms she held two babies bundled in pink-and-blue blankets; one wore a pink hat, the other blue. Meeks stood with his back to his family, looking out the window.

"Oh, my…" Felicia said, unable to control her tears.

"Those two are perfect," Farrah added.

"Actually…" Meeks turned to face his family. He, too, held another baby wrapped in a pink-and-blue blanket and wearing a blue cap. "These *three* are perfect."

"What the—?"

"Farrah…" Felicia admonished, wiping away her tears.

"Surprise!" Francine said, scanning her sisters' faces. "See, I told you they didn't know."

"Yes, you did, my love." Meeks gently pinched her cheek.

"Meeks just knew our connection would somehow spoil the surprise," Francine explained.

"Actually, I'm surprised it didn't," Robert said, frowning.

"I know I'm one of the newest members to this family…" Griffin said, trying to keep one-year-old Alyia from jumping out of his arms to get to her new cousins. "But from what I've seen of you three's connection, that surprises me, too."

"Well, we've had a lot going on lately, not to mention the added interferences." Francine looked at her children.

She smiled and her eyes danced between her sisters. "You might as well spill."

"What?" Robert and Griffin replied in unison.

Both sisters remained silent as they glared at a smiling Francine.

Farrah turned to Robert and said, "Honey, I have a surprise for you."

Felicia captured her lip between her teeth as she patted Alyia's back; her daughter's head now on Griffin's shoulder. She looked into her husband's eyes and said, "Me, too." Felicia pulled Griffin to the corner of the room.

"What's going on?" His eyes widened.

"I've decided to build a bigger house," she said, smiling.

Griffin's eyebrows stood at attention. "A house... This is about our need for a bigger house?" he clarified.

"Yes." She patted her sleeping baby on the back. "We need more bedrooms, since our family is expanding. And when they come to visit, I want everyone to be comfortable."

"Well, if that's what you want, then that's what you shall have, my love."

"I'm thinking we should have a two-bedroom guest house on the property and in our house we need four guest rooms—"

"You want to talk about this now?" Griffin glanced over his shoulder. "Don't you think we should get back to our family?"

"We will, and this *is* about our family. I think we need at least five bedroom suites—one for us, one for Ms. Ellen, Alyia, the new baby, and since multiples seem to be our thing, we'll need an extra room just in case."

Griffin stood staring at Felicia as if he'd never seen her before. "Did you just say 'new baby'?"

Felicia smiled and shrugged. "Or babies..."

Griffin pulled Felicia into his body with his free arm.

He looked at Alyia and then Felicia. She cupped his face with her right hand, using her thumb to wipe away a lone tear. "I love you, my beautiful wife."

"I love you, too."

* * * * *

REQUEST YOUR FREE BOOKS!

2 FREE NOVELS PLUS 2 FREE GIFTS!

KIMANI™
ROMANCE

Love's ultimate destination!

SPECIAL EXCERPT FROM

(H) HARLEQUIN®

KIMANI
ROMANCE

*Reality show producer Amelia Marlow has a score
to settle with sexy Nate Reyes—and buying him at a
bachelor auction promises sweet satisfaction. But the
forty hours of community service Nate owes soon turns
into sensual and sizzling overtime... Through sultry
days and even hotter nights, Nate's surprised to find
Amelia is slowly turning his "no complications wanted"
attitude into intense attraction. And he soon discovers
that he'll do anything to prove that there's only one
perfect place for Amelia—in his arms!*

*Read on for a sneak peek at
HIS SOUTHERN SWEETHEART, the next exciting
installment in Carolyn Hector's
ONCE UPON A TIARA series!*

"You're all cloak and dagger." Nate nodded at the way
she held the menu in front of her face. "Unless you need
glasses.

The way she frowned was cute. The corners of her
mouth turned down and her bottom lip poked out. A
shoe made direct contact with his shin. "My eyesight is
perfect."

"Not just your eyesight." Nate cocked his head to get a
glimpse of the hourglass curve of her shape.

"Does your cheesy machismo usually work on women?"

Nate flashed a grin. "It worked on you last week." He regretted the words the second before he finished the *K* in week. Amelia's foot came into contact with his shin again. "Sorry. Chalk this up to being nervous."

Amelia settled back against the black leather booth. "You're supposed to be nervous?"

"Who wouldn't be?" Nate relaxed in his seat. "You breeze into town and drop a wad of cash on me just to make me do work for what you could have hired someone else to do, and much more cheaply, too."

The little flower in the center of her white spaghetti-strap top rose up and down. Even through the flicker of the flame bouncing off the deep maroon glass candleholder, he caught the way her cheeks turned pink.

"Let's say I don't trust anyone around town to do the work for me."

Don't miss HIS SOUTHERN SWEETHEART
by Carolyn Hector, available October 2016
wherever Harlequin® Kimani Romance™
books and ebooks are sold!